D0410393

HOLDING THE ACE CARD

HOLDING THE ACE CARD

A Western Duo

Lauran Paine

S SAGEBRUSH
Large Print Westerns

Copyright © 2005 by Mona Paine

First published in Great Britain by ISIS Publishing Ltd.
First published in the United States by
Five Star Westerns

Published in Large Print 2007 by ISIS Publishing Ltd.,
7 Centremead, Osney Mead, Oxford OX2 0ES
United Kingdom
by arrangement with
Golden West Literary Agency

British Library Cataloguing in Publication Data
Paine, Lauran
    Holding the ace card. – Large print ed. –
    (Sagebrush western series)
    1. Western stories
    2. Large type books
    I. Title
    813.5'2 [F]

ISBN 978-0-7531-7752-5 (hb)

Printed and bound in Great Britain by
T. J. International Ltd., Padstow, Cornwall

Table of Contents

Terror Trail

The pendulous lip of the rock overhang cast a silhouette of sylvan shade down across the walls of the Spruce Mountains and out in a pointed, arrowhead shape over the range of Reno Balfor. The rider looked up at the promontory as he swung into the shade. His eyes were frank and honest, and his face was young enough to have strength without resignation. He rode easily, mechanically breaking over with each jarring motion of his horse's lope.

Reno Balfor was a busy cowman — too busy for pleasure and too busy for sociability. Too busy, in fact, for anything that didn't insure his progress in the cow country as a cattleman. He had spent a comfortable inheritance wisely and, miraculously, was administering what he had spent with rare acumen. Still, he wasn't well known by his neighbors. He'd smile, wave, or yell a greeting, but his ranch kept him absorbed in its establishment and he seemed neither to want nor need other interests.

He swung down, unsaddled, and turned his horse loose. The powerful, functional log house with its squatty, rugged appearance was handsome to him. It

3

was like the barn, in that he'd moistened each log with his sweat and knew the strength, durability, and thickness of both house and barn.

He was frying his potatoes on one skillet, his steak on the other, when he heard a rider coming. Annoyed but not irritated, Reno walked casually over, threw the door open, and was almost bowled over by the girl who catapulted into him. He stepped back, really annoyed now, and frowned at her. She wasn't stunning — unless clear skin, a full shirt, and sturdy legs in old Levi's can be stunning. Or unless honey-colored hair, tumbling from under the worn rim of a black Stetson, and a small, freckled nose and china-blue eyes and full lips are stunning. She was handsome rather than beautiful.

Reno's frown vanished. The girl was backing off, looking at the stained flour sack he always tucked into his belt when he was cooking. There was consternation mixed with amusement on her face. "Where's the owner?"

"Lady, I'm *not* the cook," Reno answered sarcastically. He yanked the flour sack apron off hastily and revealed his sagging cartridge belt and holstered gun. "What can I do for you, besides serving as a back stop?"

"Your meat . . . ," she said, wrinkling her nose. She never got to finish. With a bellow of anguish Balfor ran for the kitchen counter. The damage was done. Too well done. He dumped both skillets into the wash bucket and looked at her, where she stood, wide-eyed, peering around the doorjamb of the door.

4

"Come in, ma'am. If I have to eat warmed-over beans because of you, the least you can do is share them with me."

"Oh, I couldn't," she said demurely, moving forward and taking the can of beans out of his hand. "It really wouldn't be proper. We *are* alone, aren't we?" She deftly put the beans in a pan and on an open burner and stirred them with a big spoon Reno had been using for the fried potatoes.

"Yes. We're alone, but what's more important, I think, is that I'm hungry."

She shook the beans vigorously before she spoke and Reno watched the startling wiggle of her hips delightedly. "You're a typical bachelor. All you think about is yourself. Your stomach, in other words."

Reno sank down on a kitchen chair beside the handmade table and cocked a quizzical glance at her. "Is that," he asked dryly, "what you darned near knocked me over to say?"

"No." Her china-blue eyes flashed over him quickly. He felt a definite shock at their brightness. "I came to tell you that Arnold Gregory's stallion is in the pasture with your mares. He must have jumped the fence. Anyway, I saw him in there as I rode by."

Balfor fought down an almost irresistible desire to swear. Irascible old Arnold Gregory, his nearest neighbor to the north, had been a thorn in his flesh ever since he had bought into the Devil's Post Pile country. Gregory had two disagreeable sons that Reno had seen at a distance, plus the mangiest bunch of half longhorns-half Durhams, wild cattle, and about as tumbledown a ranch, generally speaking, as existed in the territory. Also, he had a healthy reputation as a brawler, gunman and — it was whispered — rustler and horse thief. He was tall, lanky, all square corners with a thin sheathing of tough rawhide and a weathered face under a thatch of wild, white hair. Reno could see him very plainly without even closing his eyes. The sons were younger editions of the old man.

"That danged varmint. He'll never learn that the West has changed. Lets his stock run wild, cuts fences, won't do any range improvement work, or anything else." He shook his head back and forth like a befuddled drunk. "Someone ought to tell the old relic his kind of West is gone forever. Cattle are a business now, like everything else. I've a notion to shoot his damned stud."

The girl rummaged through two cupboards before she found plates and silverware, set the table with quick, sure movements, hashed out the beans, and sat down opposite Reno, after tossing her hat on the unused chair at one side of the table. She looked quietly at him over the table.

"That might be a bad mistake. It isn't a good idea to go around shooting other people's stallions."

Balfor should have been warned by the cool tone of her voice, but he wasn't. He ate angrily. "Oh, I wouldn't shoot the horse. It's not his fault he belongs to that old piney-woods character." He made a face. The beans were blistering hot. "But darned if I won't shag him out of the country so far it'll take Gregory a month to find him. Providin' he's still in with my horses in the morning."

The girl washed and Reno wiped. He was still furious about the stud, even after she'd thanked him for the dinner and left. It wasn't until he was turning out the lantern before crawling into his bunk that he remembered with a start that he hadn't the faintest idea who she was.

Gregory's stud was still in with Reno Balfor's mares when he rode out at dawn. The intruder was a worn-down stallion, however. He'd been courting and fighting; Reno had two younger studs in the pasture that had indulged in hit-and-run tactics all night long. He roped the horse, studied the Turkey Track brand on his right shoulder with a sour face, and started off in a long lope for the back country, leading a jaded and gaunt stallion on the end of his lariat.

It was late evening before Reno got back to his own Horseshoe brand outfit. He was dog tired and irritable. So far as he was concerned, it had been a wasted day. He ate a frugal dinner of the warmed-over beans and thought about the girl while he was doing the dishes. The chore had seemed to go so much faster when she'd been there to help him. Cute, too, in a wild, unhampered way. Faded work shirt, faded Levi's, and used-up old black Stetson, rank with dust and use. But what china-blue eyes, and what an adorable mouth. And the way she'd shaken those beans in the pan. He hung up the flour sack apron, turned out the lantern, and crawled into bed, weary but vindictively happy over what he'd done to Gregory's damned stud horse.

Reno tooled the ranch wagon into Sundown the next morning for a load of supplies. He tied up unobtrusively to a ring that hung dejectedly from a giant oak off to one side of Candless's mercantile establishment. He checked over the supplies from his list, helped load them, paid up, and started for the Mossback Saloon, pride and fraternal club of the cowmen and cowboys of the Devil's Post Pile country. He was hailed and welcomed by several men he knew, as well as Jed Hartley, owner and daytime bartender, a middle-aged man with only a fringe of hair around his ears and a truculent, scarred face.

"Beer, Reno?"

Balfor nodded. Jed poured it off, set it up, and sucked juicily on his unlit cigar. "How's the cow business?"

"Cow business is fine. It's the damned horse business that's troublin' me."

"How so?"

Reno heard the louvered doors swing inward and squeak, as they always had, when he answered. "Gregory's mangy old stud was in my horse pasture all night. I suppose I'll have a bunch of piney-woods colts next year."

"*Eeeeuuuusssggghhh!*" Jed cleared his throat lustily. Reno tossed him a mildly curious look.

"I ought to have shot the damned old cold-blooded dink, but instead I just . . ."

"*Haaakkk! Spffft!*" Jed coughed laboriously, red-faced.

8

"Just," Reno went on, "took him back in the hills and left him."

"*Speeuuwwiitt!*" Jed spat lustily and coughed again.

Balfor looked over at him frowningly. "What in hell's wrong with you, Jed? Got a . . . ?"

"Ain't a damned thing wrong with him that you shuttin' up won't cure!"

Reno turned slowly. It dawned on him that Jed Hartley's labors had been uselessly expended for his benefit. He was looking into Arnold Gregory's flinty face and over the man's shoulders, tall and bony-square, were the two Gregory boys. Jack, towheaded and squint-eyed, and Jim, black headed with prominent, high cheek bones that accentuated, rather than hid, his angry eyes sunken back in their deep pockets.

"Where's m'stud horse, ya damned horse thief?" That was strong talk in the Devil's Post Pile country. The few patrons of the saloon moved off, but were loath to leave so promising a situation. Balfor felt his blood warming under the old scoundrel's belligerent stare.

"He's where he won't bother other folks' mares for a while."

Jim, younger of the two Gregory boys, stepped around in front of his father. His fists were clenched to match the hardness in his eyes. "By Gawd, *hombre*, when you're asked a civil question, answer the same way!"

Reno looked him up and down as he answered. Jim was a head taller and six inches broader than he was.

"If you call bein' called a horse thief a civil question, then you're more used to it than I am."

Jim Gregory roared an oath and leaped at Balfor. One great, long arm flew out like a cudgel, missed by two feet, and dropped away. Reno danced aside, spurs jingling frantically as Jed Hartley's voice rose over the ruckus.

"Here, now, Gregory! By Gawd there'll be none o' that. This here's a fair fight an' it's goin' to stay thataway!"

Reno risked a glance and saw the short-barreled shotgun resting on the bar and pointing directly at Arnold and Jack. He was thankful for Jed's assistance. Jim rushed him, took two jarring slams into the body, and stood off, wide-legged and furious. Reno feinted the youth, who went for it good and tried to close again. Balfor's left came overhand and stopped the cowboy, then his right came sizzling in with the whole weight of his body behind it. Jim went over backward as if he'd been hit by a tree, and collapsed at his father's feet.

Reno was blowing, but his blood was up. He faced Jack Gregory with a sneer. "You next, ya unwashed offspring of a piney-woods rustler?"

Jack sidled forward, furious and white-lipped, but Arnold Gregory grabbed his rumpled shirt from behind and yanked him back. He glowered at Reno.

"God damn' brawler, ain't ya? Real fightin' man, eh? I wish to Gawd I was twenty years younger. I'd break your damned neck for ya. Think you're pretty smart, don't ya? Comin' into this country an' settin' up as a cowman." The old man bobbed his head up and down

10

significantly. "Well, I'm goin' to teach you a few things, neighbor. Things you never heard of before!"

Reno's breath was coming easily and naturally again. He smiled dourly. "Like what, old-timer? Stealin' cattle an' rustlin' horses an' bushwhackin'?" He looked balefully at the straining son. "Turn the skunk loose, Gregory. I'd just as soon whip the whole unwashed batch of you now and get it over with, so I won't have to wash but once, when I'm through."

Jim Gregory growled deeply in his chest. Arnold was white-faced. "I ought to kill you for that, you son-of- . . ."

"Go ahead, old-timer. You got a gun."

It was Jim Gregory's turn to grab and hang on. Arnold's gun hand was straining under his son's grip. Balfor really didn't want to use his gun against old Arnold at all. He watched the murder die out of the older man's face, and then he turned with a snort of contempt and walked back to the bar. Jed Hartley was stowing the shotgun under the counter, grim faced.

"Another beer, Jed."

Hartley set it up, leveled the foam with a thick finger, and watched the Gregorys leave the saloon, then sighed shakily. "Son, you sure can fight." He picked up his unlit, scraggly-ended cigar where he'd put it when the trouble started, and rolled it around to get it warm and slippery again, between his worn teeth. "But, Gawd Almighty, boy, you sure got three bad 'uns to watch now, for sure. I wouldn't put nothin' past 'em, son. Nothin'."

For three days, things on the ranch were peaceful and routine, then Reno Balfor found his fence cut where he'd run in eighty head of yearling steers to finish on new grass before he sent them to slaughter. He knew what had happened and it made him fighting mad. He wanted those steers left alone so they wouldn't move off any weight. Gregory had known this, too. Reno found their tracks and followed them into the forested hills that backed his range. He cursed lividly as he saw where they'd been taken up the hill onto the frighteningly narrow trail that led into the back country. It was all uphill, which meant his steers would sweat off at least 100 pounds each in shrinkage.

Unmindful of the hour or the surroundings, Balfor rode along behind his stolen animals, tracking them in fuming rage. Gregory was going to wish he'd never touched those cattle!

It was close to sundown before Reno heard the protesting bellow of a critter far ahead. He left off following tracks and spurred on. Clearings showed up, small at first, then larger and knee deep in succulent, untouched grass. Suddenly, through the trees, he saw several red backs up ahead. Drawing his six-gun, he loped at an angle until he could see the right ribs of the critters. Sure enough, they were his Horseshoe steers.

Recklessly mad, Reno rode among the startled cattle and noticed that they dripped saliva and were red-eyed with exhaustion. He tried to see into the shadows, searching for riders, but couldn't find any. Then he got crafty. The Gregorys would have to return to the lowlands the same way they had gotten up, over Terror

Trail, the inches-wide slit that hugged around the rocky cliff for 100 yards. If he couldn't find them in the dusky gloom, he'd surely be able to waylay them on the trail. He turned abruptly and rode back the way he had come.

The moon was high and yellowish when Reno left his horse at the lower end of the trail, walked back to where the big lip hung out over the path, and sat down on a rock, examining his carbine and .45. They were both loaded and ready. He wanted to roll a cigarette, but was afraid the Gregorys would smell it. This slight irritation fed the fumes and fires of his anger further. By the time he heard horses coming back down the trail, he was in a killing mood. Still, he felt a sensation of exultation, too. Now these pineywoods ranchers would learn not to trifle with Reno Balfor!

The horses were still hidden by the darkness but their jingling sounds and hoof falls came distinctly downwind to him. There were three horses, which would be Jim, Jack, and Arnold. Fine. He'd sail into all three of them and instill respect once and for all, and then this bickering would be settled for all time.

Reno was so intent on the coming riders that he failed to hear the other horse, at first. When he did distinguish its walking gait behind him, on the far, lower end of the trail, he jumped up off the rock with an oath.

The newcomer, whoever he was, would arrive on the scene about the time he opened up on the Gregorys. He looked anxiously both ways. Should the fourth rider turn out to be a friend of the Gregorys, he was in a hell of a predicament there, between two fires. He was swearing with feeling and perplexity, when the first of the Gregorys appeared like an animated silhouette, coming toward him single file. It was Jack, with Jim next, and old Arnold bringing up the rear.

Reno fumed and raged inwardly, his fingers playing nervously with the cocked carbine, then he decided to throw caution to the wind. He was on Terror Trail for a purpose, and odds of four to one weren't much worse than odds of three to one, especially since he had the brief but important element of surprise in his favor.

He threw the Model 1894 to his shoulder, drew a long careful bead on Jim Gregory's peaked Stetson, and squeezed the trigger. A jagged, wild tongue of orange flame leaped out into the darkness like a finger. Gregory's hat jumped off its owner's head violently and sailed into the night. A wild, frantic oath thundered out of the gloom and Reno levered up for a second shot. His strategy was very simple: hold the Gregorys there in the rocks until they agreed to round up and return his cattle by the only trail in and out of the back country. Balfor was now master of the Terror Trail and meant to control it with gunfire until the thieves came to his terms.

A six-gun crashed up ahead. Reno grinned bitterly. They were trying to draw his fire a second time so they'd know where he was. He looked around uneasily but the fourth horseman, the one he'd heard coming up the trail from behind him, was no longer in sight or sound. He laughed wryly to himself. The stranger had probably bolted like a doe when the night had blown up in his face with gunshots, and ridden away as fast as he could go.

Reno turned back, considerably relieved. He saw a faint outline of a man trying to scale the almost vertical wall of the craggy overhang, apparently with the intention of dropping lead down onto him. Reno smiled coldly as he knelt and rested the carbine on a huge old boulder. The climber looked like Jack. He aimed about where he figured the man's next handhold would be, and fired. A frightened cry echoed over the trail and bounced back from the wall of rock as the man, badly startled, let go his meager grip and dropped fifteen feet to the rocks of the trail proper.

For a long time after that, there was silence. Reno figured the others were looking after the fallen man. He methodically reloaded the carbine and waited. The night was cold, and the tiny stars didn't make much impression in the blackness. Nor the watery moon, either, for that matter.

An hour went by, with no sound from the bottled up Gregory clan. Balfor wondered and fidgeted. He didn't like their silence and felt eyes in the dark, peering at his back, from all over the place. It was close to two hours later, nearly midnight, when he heard a sound that shook him temporarily. The rattle of many hoofs coming down the uplands toward him!

The skunks slunk back an' got the cattle and are drivin' what they got down the trail, right at me.

He saw the shaggy beasts faintly outlined with their fuzzy white faces and briskets swinging down upon him. He snapped two rifle shots over them but the animals, knowing the way home, only hesitated, and then came on, the ones behind shoving those in front. He knew that, somewhere in among the steers, were the three deadly Gregorys, guns ready and hunting for him. He risked a glance downtrail where he'd hidden his horse and his heart sank. There, in the weak and eerie moonlight, sat a horseman. Motionless and like a statue in the gloom, barring the way of both cattle and Reno Balfor alike. He groaned out loud. If the damned fool didn't move, some critters were bound to get crowded off the trail into the sheer drop of jagged cañon below. His own retreat was cut off, also. What had started out to be a brilliant stratagem had soured and backfired.

A six-gun roared close and Reno threw himself flat behind his boulder. Another gun barked and bellowed. The old boulder shook slightly under the impact of the bullets. Reno wanted to crawl to another vantage point but he didn't dare. If they had him spotted — which they evidently did — he wouldn't dare move.

Cursing in a savage whisper, he edged around the base of the rock, drew his .45, and picked up a rider over the sights. The man cried out in more rage than pain and emptied his gun against the rock. Reno lay flat and sweated. When he next risked a peek, the cattle were streaming by, lolling their tongues and rolling their eyes at the smell of a man close by. He could have reached out and touched their hoofs, clicking and churning as they rolled past. Suddenly he had a premonition and swiveled around, glaring downtrail. A man's outline was clear against the sky, stealthily creeping up on him.

16

Balfor forgot the cattle, the lone rider at the far end of the trail, and his own imminent danger as he lunged. Desperation was driving him now. Any previous thoughts he had of humbling his enemies were lost in the fight for survival. He kicked wildly at the man's gun, felt his booted toe strike bone even as he grabbed frantically at the man's vest and knocked him down. The cattle began a bewildered, insistent lowing and Reno knew instinctively that they were confused at the smell of the lone horseman at the lower end of the trail. Even if the man moved, which Reno heartily hoped had happened, the critters would still pick up his scent and feel uneasy.

"You! Ya damned, sneakin' bushwhacker!"

The man's angry voice brought Reno back in a second. He rolled with a hard left and glared squinting through the darkness and recognized Jim Gregory. Grimly he blocked a knee.

"Yeah, you would-be rustlin' hardcase! I'll teach you damned skunks to rob decent folks." He aimed a vicious short jab and hammered it home. Jim Gregory grunted and tried to wrap his long legs around Reno, but the rancher pushed him away and stepped back, letting Jim get his balance. Gregory tried a tackle, missed, and got a murderous kick to the side of the head that left him twitching and jerking into unconsciousness. Balfor collected his six-gun and was straightening up when the night blew apart almost in his eyes. Blinded by the flash, he dropped to one knee. The slug had ripped the sleeve of his shirt from the wrist to the elbow and stung the flesh. Instinctively he knew that the gunman was coming for him and threw himself sideways barely in time to miss the descending handgun.

Through a maze of sunbursts and purple pinwheels he made out a form and stood up to meet it. Jack Gregory was coming in with balled up fists, held low. Reno Balfor knew him by his shaggy look. He went to meet him with a wild, savage attack that drove Gregory backward in a stumbling retreat. Fists flailing, guard down and ignored, Reno bore in. Jack was no match for him despite his great reach. Reno bowled him backward with a stinging left, then doubled him over, before he could catch his balance, with a lobbing right and chopped him down murderously with a series of killing lefts and rights that drove the younger man to his knees, blood dripping from his nose and mouth. Jack hung there, absorbing the punishment as long as he could, trying to regain his feet until an aimed fist blew up on the side of his head, high, and he fell forward limply.

Reno was a tattered ruin of his former self. He could feel blood trickling down his arm where the bullet had singed it. The cattle were still streaming by. He cast an anxious glance at the far end of the trail and could vaguely see that nothing was impeding the downward progress of his animals. Evidently the fourth rider had disappeared again.

Balfor looked coldly at the beaten Gregory boy, then faced away as a rider loomed up behind the last of his cattle. He didn't get a good look at the man before a gun roared. Then he turned, slowly and painfully, and

18

saw Arnold Gregory, his gun lancing another lick of flame, coming toward him. The old man's first slug had struck him a glancing blow in the hip. The reaction was sickening. He was suffused with a nauseating illness and his gun came up slowly. He was crouching when the third shot slammed past him, and the fourth struck the boulder after he had ducked down behind it.

Reno could hear the last of the Gregorys coming in after him afoot. Arnold's big, rowelled spurs rang like a funeral knell. The cattle were disappearing far down the trail. He knew he wasn't dangerously hurt, but he couldn't shake off the sensation of retching sickness long enough to force himself back upright. He knew, too, that Arnold Gregory had always lived by the gun, unlike his sons, who found fists convenient, too, and thus the old man would come onto him with lead blazing. He knew, in the silence, that old Arnold was reloading. Desperation fought with the sickness and weariness until he was back to his knees. The slashed flesh of his hip burned and stung. He cocked his .45 deliberately and raised up, supporting himself with one hand against the cold boulder.

Arnold Gregory saw him come over the boulder and jumped sideways firing as he went, with only a hope of spoiling Reno's aim and with little thought of his own accuracy, as he spun away. Reno flinched instinctively but knew Arnold's slug was away wide. He rested his gun on the rock and slowly, painfully began systematically to empty it in the direction of old man Gregory. The gaunt old cowman lay cramped behind a small granite slab that absorbed the leaden punishment but threatened to crack under the impacts. Arnold counted each shot and squirmed stiffly around the slab when Reno's sixth bullet had been spent. He was grinning like a bronco Indian buck as he sighted Balfor.

Before Arnold got off a shot, however, Reno had scooped up Jim's gun and snapped two shots that drove Arnold flying for cover with particles of granite imbedded in his face and swearing harshly. He winced each time a slug hit the slab. Finally, unable to stand the suspense, he cried out.

"Balfor? Balfor, damn yer black heart! Are my boys dead?"

"No, ya rustlin' old whelp. They're sleepin' nicely, like the kids they are, but they're not hurt, ya old bas . . ."

"Balfor? Ya dry-gulchin' coyote. Ya sneakin' bushwhackin', horny toad of a . . ."

"Aw, shuddup, ya damned old relic, or I'll come over there an' part your hair, too. Fightin' man!" Reno added scornfully, making it as much of a taunt as he could, although he felt like anything but a scornful battler just then. "Hell, the whole bunch of you aren't anythin' more than scurvy, unwashed, uncivilized, uncouth white trash!"

"Damn your heart!" It was a muffled and thick yell, redolent of strangling fury. "Stand up from behind that gawd-damned rock an' swap lead with me. Just once, ya lousy snake. Just once!" There was almost a pleading eagerness in the old man's voice.

Reno lowered his head, punched fresh shells into his own gun, and shook himself to clear his vision, then he raised up as far as he dared, leaning against the rock because his wounded hip had gone numb and wouldn't support him.

"All right, ya scurvy ol' devil. I can't stand up, but I'm as high as I can get. Come up shootin'!"

Arnold Gregory shot his long, gangling legs out quickly to push himself erect, the pebbles under his boots gave way screechingly from the scramble, and he was pitched forward, hard. His chin struck against the slab and his teeth clanged together with a sharp rattling sound that grated up into his brain as a million little white lights flashed on and off. He slumped down and swore thickly in the shocking stupor of his jolt. He had to force himself upright and gritted his jaws in the effort.

Something inside his head was screaming for him to get up fast, before Balfor walked over, stuck a gun in his ear, and blew him to kingdom come. He tried, too, with every ounce of his tough old strength, to worry away the fog that was sweeping like a drug through his tattered body, but he couldn't make it until he heard the crunching sound of someone coming toward him, then he raised up with a burst of final energy and fired by instinct.

Someone yelled crazily and Arnold Gregory felt a little of the fog being torn away. Then he heard a gun go off again, at the same time his own hand and arm were torn violently sideways, spinning him around and dumping him unceremoniously half out from behind his slab. Gregory knew in a fraction of a second it was all over. He tensed and waited for the final shot that would complete Reno Balfor's victory over the house of Gregory. He knew it was coming as surely as he knew anything,

21

and, when it didn't come, he wasn't too grateful at being spared — that was an even worse insult.

Arnold twisted his head slowly and glared over at Balfor's rock. A mighty hiss of air went out of him as gradual consciousness returned. Reno Balfor wasn't going to shoot. In fact, it was doubtful if he even remembered the humbled, beaten man on the ground. Arnold pushed himself up incredulously and wiped the sharp pieces of granite out of his palms.

"Where'd you come from?"

Reno's gun dangled from his fingers. He was grinning wryly at the slim, full-figured girl with the wild eyes and tousled honey-blonde hair, who was standing in front of his rock, between him and old Gregory. Her carbine was sagging badly, but the quivering set of her mouth wasn't indicative of anything but resolve. Reno dropped his gun, grabbed the boulder with both hands, and forced himself upright. It just wasn't decent, kneeling behind the damned rock, when he was talking to anything as breathtaking and surprising as the girl with the china-blue eyes. She watched his glassy-eyed agony as he got up, gulped prodigiously, and reached over to steady him.

"Why did you do it?"

"Do it! Lady, what the hell! These are the damned, skulkin' Gregorys. Does that mean anything to you? They're the ones that owned the stud you told me was with my mares. An' now." He pointed proudly to the two men behind him who were reluctantly returning to the land of wakefulness. She leaned over soberly and looked at Jack and Jim. "And now, ma'am, they were rustlin' my cattle, an' I caught 'em and whipped them to a fare-thee-well."

"You're a damned liar!" Arnold's voice was shrill and shaking with reactivated wrath. He was limping across the trail shaking a gnarled finger at Reno. The rancher picked up his gun and tried to twist past the girl's body. She moved to block him.

"Let me get one crack at that damned old piney-woods billy goat, ma'am. Step aside. Just one shot, by Gawd."

Arnold was glaring down at him from beside, and a little behind, the girl. Reno tried to get around, where the girl wasn't in the way, but old Gregory howled and stamped his booted feet — and stayed securely behind the girl.

"We never stoled yore damned cattle, anyway."

"You never? Why, that's what you've been doin' all afternoon, ya lyin' old devil. Drivin' my cattle back into the . . ."

"Sure we drove 'em. Just like you drove our stud horse off. But we was just goin' to leave 'em back there for you to find for yourself, just like you did us. We weren't stealin' a single head, not on your battlin' heart we wasn't. Ask the boys, by Gawd. They'll . . ."

"Yeah," Reno howled back at him, "they'll say anythin' you tell 'em." He looked down dubiously at the squatting Gregorys behind him. "Besides, you unwashed old coot, they're damned well cured of botherin' me, I think, unless they want to get the livin' hell beat out of them again."

He glared at the old man, his eyes flaming with fury, and saw the calm, watching look of the girl, and blushed. She wasn't saying a word. Just standing there, hiding that old hulk of a wild-eyed Arnold Gregory, so small and so, well, so damned cute and sort of, well, sort of lovable.

"Reno Balfor, when I told you about the Gregory stud being in with your horses, I thought we'd go both together and cut him out, rope him, and I'd take him home."

"Home?" An awful, incredulous, horrifying thought built up inside his head. "Home, ma'am? Where?"

"Home to the Turkey Track, Reno Balfor. Home with me to the Turkey Track. But then, well, we had dinner an' it got dark, an' . . ."

"*You* had dinner with *him*?" Arnold Gregory's ashen face was a study in tremendous shock and terror. "With *him*, Judy? In his cabin, girl?" Her china-blue eyes were brimming and her full mouth was weakening against the assaults of quivers that lay in the muscles behind it. She stood there, half turned away from Reno, looking up into the terribly shocked old face of Arnold Gregory, and nodded.

"Yes, Dad. It wasn't . . . well, we sort of both got hungry, Dad. It didn't take long. I mean, I only stayed a little while . . ."

Reno's surprise vanished before the pathos of Judy Gregory. He shook his head unbelievably, glaring from father to daughter.

"You must've stolen her, or adopted her, or something. You never could've had anything like . . ."

"You shut up!" Judy's eyes, with their brimming load of hot tears stinging them, flamed at him like blue ice.

24

"You keep your mouth closed! I've heard about all I want to hear of the way you talk about my family. My dad's *not* unwashed, an' he's *not* a piney-woods ol' coot." A sob stole up and choked her for a second. Reno reached down and took her gun. She let him take it when their hands met. He turned owlishly and pointed it at the brothers.

"Get around in front of this rock, damn you!" They got — fast! "Now, look here. I'll whip you one at a time, two at a time, or, gawd damn it, three at a time, anytime you want me to." Jim and Jack were keeping a healthy distance between themselves and the injured man. "But I'll be damned if I'll fight you *four* at a time." He looked away from the awed and thoroughly cowed brothers, over Judy's head to Arnold Gregory's unblinking, watching eyes. "And as for you, you old hound, you're too old for me to larrup, so I'm telling you here an' now, before witnesses an' all, that Judy's goin' to take care of me at my ranch until I can get around again, y'understand? You *hombres* are responsible for my hurts, an' damn ya, that's the least you can do. And" — Reno's eyes dropped to the china-blue ones that were watching him with something like awe — "I might even keep her there permanently . . . that is, if she'll stay. I mean . . . Judy . . . I need a wife an' you need a husband, or somethin', an' . . . an' . . . oh, damn it! Judy, I talk too much sometimes, don't I?"

Rapture stared up at him in the pink dawn. She smiled gently and shook her head. "Or not enough, Reno," she said.

Holding the Ace Card

CHAPTER
ONE

There were four men in the saloon. One of them was looking out into the roadway. The other three were at the card table with Lou Bellanger, concentrating on their game. One of them said — "Who's got openers?" — and that was as far as the game ever got. The man over at the window turned. He was solidly compact with heavy, club-like, small hands and stubby fingers. He looked straight at Lou Bellanger.

"You won't need no openers," he said, loud enough for even the barkeep to hear. "The law's coming."

Bellanger raised a caustic face to the solid man, read the antagonism there, and gently placed his cards face down. Across the table his associates were watching him, suspicion bright in their steady eyes. Tension held them motionless. Something hard settled upon the bar top off on Bellanger's right. He knew the sound and turned his head. The barkeep was pointing his backbar sawed-off riot gun straight at Lou.

Where sunlight streamed into the otherwise cool and shadowy large old room, a tall man came in out of the heat, and stopped. He had the badge, but more than that he had the look; it fell upon Lou Bellanger with a deceptive gentleness. It was one of those looks that believed nothing. It wasn't cruel or particularly hostile; it was an impersonal look, as though the sheriff were examining a strange new insect, something he'd be guarded against, but nothing he had to worry very much about.

"Stand up," he said to Lou. "And easy does it, cowboy."

Bellanger unwound up off the chair, his interest lifting with him. He thought of several things he might have said, but voiced none of them.

"One of you boys reach over and disarm him," said the sheriff. This was done by the splay-handed watcher from over by the window. He enjoyed doing it, too; he showed a cruel, little wolfish grin as he lifted out the gun and stepped back.

Bellanger knew what would come next, and it came. "Outside," ordered the sheriff, stepping to one side and jerking his head. "Walk easy now, cowboy. We're going down to the jailhouse."

Bellanger left the saloon, paused to let the tall man step up beside him, then he raised his left hand gently to squeeze his right arm, also raised, about eight inches up from the wrist. A detaining spring released the hide-out Derringer; it jumped from beneath his sleeve into his palm, and Lou Bellanger was armed again.

"Walk along," ordered the sheriff, giving Bellanger's shoulder a slight shove. "That's the jailhouse across the road an' southward. Just walk along and remember I'm back here."

Bellanger shuffled across the road, stood poised until a red-wheeled runabout spun past, then headed for the opposite sidewalk. There were plenty of people out; it was early afternoon. There were several wagons and a number of horsemen passing back and forth, too. No one seemed to suspect that Bellanger was a prisoner, probably because the lawman stayed a long ten feet back. But all the same, there were too many people, so Bellanger strolled right on down to the jailhouse, pushed open the door, and stepped inside. That was when he spun around on the balls of his feet and caught the sheriff flat-footed. He cocked the little .41-caliber Derringer.

The sheriff's lips flattened on his teeth. A ripple of muscle danced along on either side of his face. Bellanger stepped aside for the sheriff to come farther into the room. He did; he hiked across to his desk, turned his back on Lou, and flung down his hat. Then he turned, looking furious. Even his ears were red.

"I ought to make you eat that damned thing," he growled, but made no move away from the desk.

Bellanger held out his hand, his free hand, for the lawman to hand him back his six-gun. Not a word passed between them until Bellanger had the six-gun back in its holster. Then he stepped to a chair, swung it, dropped astraddle of it, and pocketed his .41 Derringer. "Sit," he said.

The sheriff was balanced upon the knife edge of a bad decision and, for as long as it took him to make up his mind, he didn't sit. Bellanger sat there, watching and waiting. When he seemed to believe the sheriff might try something, he shook his head.

"Sit," he said again.

31

That time the lawman loosened, turned, kicked the chair around, and dropped down upon it. He had seen the growing determination in the younger man's expression evidently, which probably made up his mind for him more than anything else.

"You're Bellanger," he said, spitting out the name. "Lou Bellanger. I've been waiting five days for you to show up in Brigham. You may think that Derringer fixed it so's you'll ride out, but nothing like that can happen. I'm not the only one, Bellanger."

"Yeah," retorted the younger man. "I got that impression over at the saloon. All right, now tell me . . . why?"

The sheriff made a cold grin. He was a man in his tough forties who'd come to manhood in a harsh environment. At an early age he'd had to learn to judge other men, and make those judgments fast. He was a single man, and a hard one, but along with that he was shrewd and wise. He said: "Bellanger, you call it and I'll arrest you for it. Stage robbery, horse stealin', rustling, safe blasting."

The younger man smiled at the sheriff without saying a word. He got up to disarm the sheriff, afterward to stand sideways so he could watch the lawman at the same time as he looked through a window out into the pitilessly sun-brightened roadway.

"Not a chance," murmured the lawman again. "Bellanger, you might as well quit right now. They're out there. Some of 'em are waitin' in the doorways, some behind store windows. Down at the livery barn there are three of the best ones. 'Course, you didn't

32

leave your critter at the livery barn like I figured, but that won't matter now. The men you were playing cards with will spread the word."

"That's what I'm gambling on, Sheriff," said Bellanger. "That they'll spread the word that you got me under lock and key." He turned from the window. It was going to be a long wait until sundown. "After five days your posse men are bored. After hearing you got me, they're going to chuck the waiting game."

Bellanger dropped the bar behind the roadside door, seated himself across the room where he had a full view, and began poking the bullets out of each opening in the sheriff's six-gun cylinder. There were two steel cells along the north wall, both empty. There was a little potbellied stove in the southwest corner of the room, also empty. A few splinters of kindling wood in a box beside the little stove were left over from wintertime. It could get rattling cold in Arizona in wintertime no matter what anyone said. Bellanger finished with the gun and tossed it. As the lawman caught it, he said: "Put it in your holster, Sheriff. If anyone got in here, it'd look better if you seemed armed." Bellanger leaned back, his blue eyes humorous. He was a lanky man in his late twenties with a mane of coarse blond hair that had a sort of cowlick right in front. He looked like a good-natured, sinewy cowboy, not an outlaw. Although it was rumored no gunfighter in Arizona Territory could draw against Lou Bellanger, to look at him, to watch him ambling around, or sitting all in a sprawl as he now was in the sheriff's office, it seemed too preposterous for credence.

He said: "Sheriff, what's your name?"

"Bob Nichol."

"Bob, how did you learn, a week back, I was coming to Brigham?"

Nichol shook his head. "I'll tell you the truth, but you're not going to believe it. I got an unsigned letter, mailed from Vernal, Utah."

Lou's eyes drew out narrowly, remaining steadily upon the peace officer. "Yeah I believe you," Bellanger replied quietly. "What did you do with the letter?"

Sheriff Nichol turned and nodded in the direction of the stove. Bellanger followed this gesture and afterward said: "You care to know why I believe you, Bob? Because I was in Vernal a week back. In fact, I spent nearly a month there with one of the prettiest little taffy-haired Mormon girls you ever saw in your life. She had eyes as blue as cornflowers and skin the color of new gold. When she smiled, a man's heart near stopped, an', when she laughed . . . Bob . . . when she laughed, it was like all the music in kingdom come comin' to life just over your shoulder."

Sheriff Nichol looked skeptical. He'd been a bachelor all his life. He'd seen his share of handsome females. In fact, years back Bob Nichol had even sparked a heifer or two. But somehow he'd gotten through into his forties without any permanent alliances, and now, with the sound judgment of maturity, his view of handsome females was best kept to himself, especially around anyone as young and obviously impressionable as Lou Bellanger.

But Lou surprised him. He smiled at Sheriff Nichol and said: "You'd just never guess her to be the least bit interested in that two thousand reward dead or alive for Lou Bellanger, Bob, until you looked deep into her sky-blue eyes . . . and saw the avarice, the naked, raw greed."

Nichol said tartly: "Then you shouldn't be surprised I was expecting you, Bellanger."

"Sheriff, I wasn't surprised." Bellanger smiled. "Wasn't surprised at all." He held up his right arm. "You don't think I go around all the time wearing one of these silly spring holsters up my sleeve, do you?"

Nichol sat perfectly still, gazing across the room. His face assumed a sour expression and his eyes shone with strong dislike. "Are you sayin' you rode into Brigham knowin' I'd arrest you?"

"Sheriff, I rode into Brigham hopin' you'd arrest me. That's why I didn't leave my horse at the livery barn, why instead I headed straight for that saloon. That's also why I came in mid-afternoon when the bars wouldn't be full." Lou tapped his right forearm again. "And this thing, Sheriff, that's why I was wearin' this thing. To do just exactly what I did. Bob, I got no hankerin' to go to prison. I didn't figure to fight. At least not until I was alone in the jailhouse with whoever arrested me. That's why I bought this spring holster off a gunsmith up in Vernal before comin' down here."

Sheriff Nichol digested all this in stony silence. His skepticism, though, evaporated. He believed Bellanger, and that only made it all the more difficult to sort out, so he said: "Why?"

35

The young gunfighter ambled over to look out the window again to study the reddening sky of early evening, the dwindling roadway traffic, and the store fronts over across the way. "Can't tell you that," he finally answered, swinging to lean his wide shoulders upon the rough wall.

"If it's for some scheme in the Brigham country, Bellanger," exclaimed Sheriff Nichol, "you'll be wise to forget it! I've let half the countryside know that you're coming here. You wouldn't be able to close your eyes at night nor turn your back to the trees in daylight."

Bellanger studied Nichol, saw in him the tough, brave, narrow, dogmatic type individual a man had to be to fulfill the requirements of a cow-town lawman. A man reasoned with the Bob Nichols of this world from behind a gun, as Lou was doing now, or he knuckled under to them because, right or wrong, the Bob Nichols were uncompromising. A bullet changed their minds, but that was all that ever did, or that ever could change them.

As an enemy, men like Nichol were dangerous for just one characteristic: they never gave up. They clung to a trail like leeches; they hunted a man with iron resolve; they battered and badgered and persevered until someone turned in snarling frustration and shot them down — or got shot down by them.

Some lawmen could be kidded out of making trouble, or persuaded, or even bought, but not men like Sheriff Bob Nichol. Lou stopped smiling and looked to see how rapidly dusk was coming, then he turned back and said: "Bob, it's goin' to make you look bad, me walking out of here tonight. I can't help that. I came to Brigham for a damned good reason. While we're sort of friends here this evening, I'm going to tell you something. A personal reason brought me here. Not pay. I'm not going to cause you grief if I can help it, beyond this embarrassment tonight. Don't go tearin' up the countryside, Bob, or you might force a killing. Why I'm here isn't goin' to bother you at all, unless you force it."

CHAPTER
TWO

Of course, the trouble with Lou Bellanger's logic was simply that people were stunned initially, then outraged, when they learned the following morning that Lou Bellanger had escaped.

"Had a dog-goned hide-out gun up his sleeve," reported Elmer Beadle, day barman over at the Trail Saloon. "Seems to me a feller who'd been at the law game as long as Bob Nichol should have figured something like that. After all, Lou Bellanger isn't just *any* outlaw."

Bell Forrester, the solidly built man who'd been keeping the vigil at the Trail and who'd signaled Sheriff Nichol, when Lou was comfortably engrossed in his poker game, through that dirty front window, said a peace officer was entitled to the co-operation of folks, for a fact, but that folks were surely entitled to something besides a damned fool for a lawman, too.

"Now that he's loose, I an' some of the other boys who helped round him up might just as well make our wills, or leave the country. From what I've heard of Bellanger, he never forgets an enemy."

Sam Chavez, the saddle and harness maker, a coffee-colored individual with startling blue eyes, was older than most and because of his monkish trade — he worked entirely alone day in and day out — made perhaps the best observation of them all. Over a glass of ale up at the Trail half-Mexican Sam Chavez said: "A man gets lots of time to think in my business, to wonder about people and things. Bellanger didn't hurt no one. He didn't even hit Bob over the head or steal a horse, or rob anyone. Oh, I know what folks say. I've heard all those stories, too. But you know, I'm sixty years old. I've just got old enough to figure something out. A man should judge another man, not by what folks say of him, but by how he treats *you*. I don't think Lou Bellanger is here for trouble with Brigham, or any of us. Not even with Bell Forrester for turnin' him in like that. For my part, I'm goin' to sit back an' watch an' wait."

Elmer Beadle swiped over the bar top with his sour rag and said pointedly: "Sam, that's all right for you to say. You ain't Bell Forrester nor me. Hell, I'm the feller threwed down on Bellanger with my shotgun. You can't hardly figure a man's goin' to like havin' you do that to him."

"Sometimes," murmured old Sam blandly, "if a feller figures out ahead what might happen *after* he does something, he's better off than just decidin' on the spur of the moment to do it."

Among the range men there wasn't this same unanimity of feeling. For one thing, northern Arizona had been popular for almost a generation for precisely one reason. It was handy to Utah for hard-pressed Arizonans and it was, conversely, handy to Arizona for shady Utahans. The cow camps and big ranches were respectable now, even Bob Nichol said that, but there had been a time when more than one cow ranch was founded upon gold fortunes that had come into their owner's hands by some very bizarre and rapid methods.

Range riders, too, were a rough, wary-eyed brotherhood in the northern Arizona country up around the town of Brigham. Mostly they chuckled over the escape of Lou Bellanger, and made sly, little, quiet remarks against Bob Nichol.

But as all things eventually do, this talk atrophied after a week or two, because nothing happened. No stages were stopped, no steel safes dynamited, no cow buyers robbed. Folks didn't forget that Lou Bellanger had been in the Brigham country. A few men, like Elmer Beadle at the Trail Saloon and Bell Forrester who was a kind of straw boss at one of the Mexican Hat cow camps, jumped every time someone slammed a door or stamped a foot, but generally folks said Lou Bellanger had left the country.

He did, in fact, leave the Brigham country. Lou left it the same night he broke out of Bob Nichol's jailhouse. And he stayed out of it for a week, which was during the height of all the excitement. Then, as the talk dwindled, Lou returned, and that was exactly why he returned when he did, because common sense said the best time for a man to get scarce was right at the height of the excitement, and, if he had to return, the time for that was when something else came along to turn the attention away from him, or else when the excitement just plain petered out for lack of sustaining force.

40

But there'd been a good reason, aside from wishing not to be too close by when the excitement arose over his escape, for Lou to ride up the northward stage road. He had a rendezvous to keep. The trouble with this rendezvous was that, although Lou knew the place and the approximate time to be there, he had no idea when the man he was to meet would show up. All Lou was certain of was that he would show up. After all, an individual as capable and shrewd as Two-Gun Jim London kept his word. That was part of the pride of the man. Lou had heard plenty about Jim London's pride, too, so he whittled the letter B on a juniper tree beside the stage road where the big white rock stood to let London know Bellanger was around, then he withdrew a mile or so back into the rough sagebrush hills, made his camp near a seepage spring, and sat down to wait.

That was what kept him out of the Brigham country and gave rise to the rumor that he'd pulled out after escaping. Even Bob Nichol, returning with four men from his last long hunt, dusty, aching, parched, and bone-dry, gave it as his opinion that Lou Bellanger was gone.

Then Bob had a bath, cleaned up his clothes, ate supper, and drifted up to the Trail to drink alone at the far end of the bar in an atmosphere of solid discomfort, and privately reflect upon the things Lou had told him. Things that convinced Bob that Bellanger in fact hadn't left the country, that he was just holing up until the noise and hubbub died down.

One thing in particular troubled Bob Nichol. Even though he'd been almost positive that girl up in Vernal,

Utah had secretly informed Sheriff Nichol the notorious Lou Bellanger was heading for Brigham, Bellanger still rode into town. That was as contrary to anything Sheriff Nichol had ever before experienced with an outlaw as he could imagine. It just didn't make sense. Even granting Bellanger had expected to be taken, had, in fact, coolly and practically provided himself with counter-steps against it, nevertheless Bob Nichol couldn't imagine what could draw a man like Bellanger to the Brigham country when it was an even chance he'd be shot on sight instead of just trapped alive.

Nerve, Bob told himself, over his second drink, ice-cold nerve. But still, even granting it was this nerve, there still had to be a reason behind it. What? There was no trouble that Bob knew of around the countryside, no trouble, at least, which would require a professional gunman. And the girl up in Vernal who'd written Bob that Bellanger was coming — her sole interest, of course, was the blood money she'd collect if Bellanger had been killed, or at the very least sent to prison. Over his third drink Bob got to thinking back to — ". . . eyes as blue as cornflowers and skin the color of new gold . . ." — and made a bitter smile into the backbar mirror at himself. It was enough to make the saliva in the back of a man's throat curdle. Eyes as blue as cornflowers, indeed!

Finally, signaling for his last nightcap, Nichol asked himself the biggest riddle of all: why had Bellanger told the girl in Vernal, Utah he was coming down to Brigham, Arizona? Bellanger had sat right there in

42

Bob's jailhouse, smiling into Bob's eyes while telling him that he knew it was the girl who'd betrayed him. And he'd kept right on smiling. That, in Bob Nichol's view, was the damnedest riddle of it all.

He had his last drink and departed. A few skeptical glances followed him on out, but not many. Enough time had passed for the escape of notorious Lou Bellanger to begin losing its earlier tingle and suspense.

Merritt Burgess, who ran the big mercantile establishment with headquarters in Brigham, was concluding a quiet, solemn conversation with a pair of weather-checked cowmen on the sidewalk when Sheriff Nichol left the Trail. All three of those older men turned and wordlessly considered Nichol. He saw them, too, and saw their shadowy, grave faces in the speckled night. Bellanger had been right about one thing; his escape was causing Nichol some embarrassment.

"Bob!" called Burgess, who was a large, heavy man with a heavy gold watch chain draped across an ample gut and a head of wiry iron gray hair. "Bob, just a second."

Nichol waited, fishing for a cigar he'd bought in the saloon. He lit it behind cupped hands, snapped the match, and saw, from the corner of his eye, Burgess's two friends enter the saloon.

"Bob," Burgess said, turning southward to walk with the sheriff, "folks are sayin' Bellanger got clean away."

"Looks that way," Nichol replied a trifle coldly. "I tracked out every fresh sign and came up with nothing." He paced along, smoking, not looking around at his companion at all. For Bob Nichol, the most irritating thing was for outsiders to butt into his vocation with their advice and their mealy criticisms. Bob Nichol had never accepted the fact that all holders of public office are prime targets for anyone and everyone. He didn't accept it now. He said: "Merritt, have you ever lost money on a sour account?"

Burgess turned his head. "Every businessman has at some time or another."

"More than one, Merritt?"

"Of course, more than one."

"Then let me tell you something, Merritt. Lou Bellanger is the first prisoner I've ever lost out of a jailhouse, and I've been a lawman twenty years, which means I've handled hundreds of badmen."

Burgess accepted this oblique squelch with his head lowered as he strode along with the sheriff. He was a wealthy man, but for all that Burgess wasn't intolerant or overbearing. He eventually said in a mild tone of voice: "Bob, I'm not criticizing. It's simply that as chairman of the town council I'm goin' to have to take a stand one way or another."

Nichol stopped and turned, his cigar belligerently tipped upward between clenched teeth. "What stand?" he demanded. "Whether to fire me or not? Merritt, I've seen that tried before. Let me tell you how it works. Sheriffs are elected countywide. Town councils can't fire them. The best you can do is hire a town marshal to keep order here in Brigham, but I'm still county peace officer. The only way you can get me out is by recall petition, and that takes a two-thirds majority of signatures to recall me from office."

Nichol stepped around Merritt Burgess out into the shadowy roadway and started stiffly stamping over toward the jailhouse. His shoulders were stiff, too, and his head rode atop his neck as though anger were the only emotion he could feel right then. It may have been. In fact, it probably was, for otherwise the assassin wouldn't have gotten away scotfree.

Nichol was slightly more than halfway across. There were no coal-oil street lamps in Brigham like some frontier towns possessed. In fact, down in the neighborhood of the jailhouse there were no lights at all, because the lighted saloon and card room was northward, up near the other end of town. The moon was up there, but Brigham's false-fronted buildings cast black shadows. Starlight didn't help much, either, except perhaps to give the assassin his light for aiming.

Merritt was standing back where Nichol had left him, half indignant, half chagrined. He didn't see a thing until the flash of flame lanced out from between two buildings across the way. Even then he was half blinded and totally stunned. He saw Sheriff Nichol swing sideways as though wrenched away by an invisible hand. He saw Nichol go down in the churned dust of the roadway. He stood there until someone's high shout out front of the Trail Saloon slammed into his brain, bringing him back down to reality. Then, with a gasp, he ran forward. It never occurred to Merritt Burgess there would be another shot. He wasn't armed; he hadn't carried a firearm in twenty years.

Blood lay like shiny black oil in the dirt. Merritt got heavily down on one knee and eased Nichol over onto

45

his back. The sheriff was as limp as a broken doll. He was breathing, but in a shallow, fluttery manner.

Two range men came running up, their spurs making musical sounds. One of them had his gun palmed; this one seemed just as interested in the possibility of the assassin still being around as he was in dropping down beside Sheriff Nichol. Other men came, too. By that time it was clear there would be no second shot. One of the cowboys said: "Is he dead?"

Merritt shook his head. "Pick him up. We'll take him over to Doctor Hart's house."

A man who'd just arrived, breathing hard and looking up and down through the gloom, said: "Bellanger! It was Bellanger!"

Merritt raised his eyes, until this moment unconcerned with who had done it. The range man saw that look. He gestured with a cocked six-gun.

"Did you see him, Mister Burgess?"

"No," said Merritt, grunting to his feet to assist in carrying Nichol away. "And neither did you, Bell. I was standing right over there in front of my store. Bob and I had just finished talking. All I saw . . . and I was closest . . . was the flash of the gun from between two buildings."

"It was Bellanger all the same!" exclaimed Bell Forrester, putting up his gun and twisting toward the gathering, solemn-faced crowd. "Who else would it have been?"

No one argued against this theory, but here and there among the hard-faced range men there was a glimmer of doubt, or at least of withheld judgment.

They carried Sheriff Nichol up the dusty roadway through patches of light and dark toward a neat bungalow with a weathered shingle nailed to the front gate announcing that **Conrad Hart, Doctor of Homoeopathic Medicine,** resided within, and there, while four men, including panting, badly upset Merritt Burgess, trooped through the gate and up toward the porch, the majority of men remained beyond the little picket fence.

Bell Forrester said it again. "It was Bellanger all right an', if enough of us get astride right now an' fan out, this time we'll catch a damned murderer. He can't be more'n a half mile away, an' us fellers know this country. Come on, who's with me?"

They were all with him. Even the ones who had doubts about Bellanger returning just to pot-shoot Bob Nichol. Those doubters went along for a better reason; they knew that whoever had shot Nichol, Bellanger or someone else, still couldn't be too far away.

CHAPTER
THREE

Maybe the assassin wasn't very far off, but Bell Forrester's posse didn't find him, and by morning they'd made so many tracks of their own trying to find him, it was useless to start over fresh and track him down.

Bell had to go back to his Mexican Hat cow camp. The other range men also had to head for their bunkhouses and camps, which left the mess in the hands of the townsmen. Some of them had been cowboys in years past, so they were qualified enough to ride as posse men, but not a one of them, stockman or townsman, knew the first thing about apprehending an assassin unless they could run him down and wring a confession from him.

The town council met in the storeroom of Merritt Burgess's big mercantile establishment shortly after noon of the day following the assassination, and except for stating it as a fact that Sheriff Nichol wasn't dead yet, although Conrad Hart didn't give him much of a chance for survival, they hadn't much to say. Merritt summed it up. "Maybe it was Bellanger, like Bell Forrester said, but I saw the gun flash, and I was closest when it happened, and I tell you I didn't see even the shape of that bushwhacker over there in the darkness. One minute Bob was walking across the road toward his office, the next moment there was that explosion, and Bob was down in the road, for all the blessed world like he was dead."

Of course, up at the Trail, and even over the café counters, the forges of the smithies in town, around kitchen tables where the ladies met to drink coffee and unmercifully dissect people who weren't present when they held these little gatherings, the talk was of Lou Bellanger. Elmer Beadle's wife, a frowsy, sagging woman with too-small blue eyes set too closely together, said that her husband, who was in a position to know, had confided in her that Bellanger had not only shot Sheriff Nichol, but had been imported into the Brigham country to assassinate someone else. About this second victim's identity, Mrs. Beadle would only roll her little pig-like eyes and make all her fat quiver in breathless anticipation. But that story spread as rapidly as the others, and for several days there was a dearth of customers in town.

The way Lou Bellanger learned that Sheriff Nichol had been shot was quite by accident. He'd left his pleasant little secret place near the seepage spring to go down closer to the juniper tree and white rock, keeping his vigil for Two-Gun Jim London, when the southbound stage out of Utah whisked past and someone casually threw aside a little newspaper published north of the line. Lou went down on foot, retrieved the paper, took it back up atop his brushy knoll, and settled down to kill time, reading.

The story of Sheriff Nichol's assassination was luridly detailed across the front page. In a separate column some clever journalist who'd visited Brigham detailed with minute care all the marshaled facts that supported Bell Forrester's contention that the shooting had been perpetrated by none other than the notorious gunfighter, Lou Bellanger, who'd been in Brigham — had, in fact, escaped from Sheriff Nichol's jailhouse — only a week or so earlier, then had, so the account said, murderously crept back under cover of a moonless night and had fiendishly laid in wait to perpetrate his dastardly and inhuman act. It was all there, including the eyewitness accounts of Nichol's lying in the dark roadway. The only thing really lacking was any actual statements of identification of the assassin. In fact, merchant Merritt Burgess said he'd been the only one present at the time of the shooting, and he'd seen nothing but the flash of the killer's weapon.

That same afternoon, while Bellanger sat atop his hill, smoking and thinking, a rider came slowly down the north roadway with his stiff-brimmed black hat tipped back, his Prince Albert coat, elegant and also dusty, unbuttoned, whistling the tune to a song called "Shenandoah". He was a man as tall as Lou Bellanger himself. But he was darker; his skin was bronzed by sunlight, and his hair was black and his eyes, up close, turned out to be a gold-flecked odd shade of brown. His features were aquiline, slightly hawkish in fact, and his mouth was long, narrow, and as straight as a bear trap.

50

Lou folded his paper, pocketed it, and sat up intently to watch the stranger. If he were Two-Gun Jim London, he would head for the juniper tree and white rock. He did.

He turned off the road, stopped in the juniper's unfragrant shade, dismounted, and stood beside his horse, looking all around. Then he made a cigarette and lighted it, as relaxed and easy as a man could be. Finally, as Lou scrambled through the brush back to where his horse patiently drowsed, stepped aboard, and reined around so as to hit the northward roadway, also, the stranger continued whistling his melancholy wartime song.

It was this whistling that kept Lou informed of the stranger's whereabouts as he urged his horse down across a brushy, rocky gulch and out of it onto the roadway. When Lou turned, working his way down the road over the stranger's fresh tracks, he also whistled a few bars of "Shenandoah". That stopped the stranger, who fell to listening. Later, when Lou hove into sight, the black-hatted man leaned across his saddle on the off side, eyeing Bellanger's slow approach.

It was a little past noon. The heat was there, but it wasn't particularly unpleasant. It was still too early in the year for that unnerving Arizona heat. As far southward as a man cared to look, the land was as clear and sharp as glass. That, also, was an advantage, at least for Bellanger whose newspaper had courteously informed him that posses had scoured the countryside for him, and would still scour it further, until he was brought to the bar of justice.

51

He reined over toward the juniper, halted, and looped his reins, genially smiling at the man in the stiff-brimmed black hat. "Hot," he said. "And it's a mighty long trail from there to here."

The dark, hawkish man smiled back, but in the way a panther might smile before striking his kill. "I like heat," he said. "I also like playing poker." He removed his black hat, fished a card from the lining, and held it up. "Ace of spades," he said.

Lou removed his hat and brought forth an identical ace of spades. Then he dismounted. "Jim London?" he asked, extending his hand. "I'm Lou Bellanger."

The dark man shook hands, his odd, gold-flecked dark eyes taking the full measure of Bellanger. "I've heard a lot about you," he said. "I reckon we'll get to know one another better down here."

Lou took London's ace of spades, bent down, and placed both their cards under the white rock. He straightened up, and shrugged. "That's what the note said to do with 'em. I reckon someone wants to be sure we met like we were supposed to. Tell me, Jim, where were you when you got your letter with the card in it?"

"Laramie. Where were you, Lou?"

"Vernal, Utah . . . with the prettiest Mormon miss you ever laid eyes on."

London took a big drag off his smoke and killed the thing underfoot. "You know who hired us?" he asked, raising his curious eyes.

"Yeah, I know. Tonight we'll ride down there."

"Why not right now? You known hereabouts?"

"I am now," said Bellanger, and fished out the flimsy little newspaper. "Mount up. I'll take you back to my camp. You can read the newspaper on the way."

Two-Gun Jim London turned, stepped up across leather, set his horse to following Lou's animal, then stretched forth the newspaper to read while he was carried along. The only time he looked around was when they began bucking their way through the thorn-pin brush. But London didn't say anything; he simply looked. He struck one as the kind of man who never said anything he didn't have to say.

They reached Bellanger's camp, off saddled, turned their animals loose upon the ankle-high good grass, and squatted in the shade of the only cottonwood tree anywhere around. London folded the paper, gravely handed it back, tossed down his hat, and lay back in the cool grass with both arms under his head.

"You cut a fat hog, didn't you?" he said. "So now you can't ride back into Brigham. Unless there's a way to boil water around here."

Bellanger looked blank. "Boil water?"

London yawned. "Yeah. Boil water to make the dye, then darken your hair an' eyebrows, and also make your hide darker if you like. It's walnut stain. I always pack a bottle of it with me. Change of clothes, change of color, hell, Lou, your own mammy wouldn't know you." London cocked one light brown eye. "You didn't really slip back down there and blast that damned sheriff, did you?"

"No."

"I didn't think so. It'd be a stupid stunt, drawing all that attention. Say, Lou . . . ?"

"Yeah."

"I'm curious about a couple of things. The letter I got over in Laramie said I'd meet you here. That was fine with me, only . . . why you in particular?"

"I'm the son," replied Bellanger, gazing steadily at London.

If he expected surprise, even a little flicker of interest, Bellanger was disappointed. Two-Gun Jim London, one of the most notorious gunfighters of all time, yawned again, scratched his nose, and made a swipe at a circling fly. "Damn but I'm bushed. I had to cover a heap of miles to get here, and even then I'm about three days late."

"Four days," corrected Bellanger.

"Yeah, four days." London sat up, propped himself upon one elbow, and made a bold, steady study of Bellanger. "You're the son," he said, repeating Lou's earlier words. "All right. Does that mean you're payin' the tab?"

"No. Well, at least so far I'm not. With me it's a personal affair. You understand, or don't those things bother you?"

London's hawkish features seemed never entirely to alter expression. Only his strange eyes changed, and that, too, was an almost imperceptible thing, just a shading that came and went so swiftly it was hardly even seen, unless a person learned to watch for it.

"I understand," he said softly. "Sure, I understand. It's just that, with me, it's never happened. It never

54

could happen, Lou. If I had any folks, I sure never knew 'em, and no one's ever told me of them, either. So you see, it couldn't happen. But I can understand it, all right." London looked over where their horses were greedily eating, then back again. "When I was a kid, I used to pack a magazine with me I found in a garbage dump back in Saint Joe. It told all about this Buckskin Bill character. It sounds crazy, I know, but I used to take that silly magazine to bed with me. Y'know, if a buffler hunter hadn't thrown the magazine in the fire one night and told me to quit having dreams like that or I'd wind up loony as a coot, I'd probably still be packin' the damned thing."

Lou had some dead brush fagots to use in making his fires. Dead, dry ones made very little scent and no smoke at all. He set about boiling some coffee and making some frypan dough cakes. As he worked, he said: "Jim, no one around Brigham's to know. If they did, when this is all over and you an' I pull out, there wouldn't be any peace left behind."

"Makes sense," agreed London, and kept studying the younger man's profile and the way he handled himself. "But there's somethin' else, Lou. How much do the folks we work for know?"

"The woman knows. That's all. But she's married and has a couple of kids. Small kids."

London dropped his eyes to the little fire inside Bellanger's stone ring. "She wrote you?" he asked.

"Yeah."

"Well. She sure as hell knows you're her son, doesn't she?"

Bellanger turned. "That's a stupid thing to say. Of course, she knows. She was right young back then, Jim. She left me to be raised by some other folks. They died. In a letter they left me, it told the whole story. When I got the letter from Brigham while I was up in Vernal, I sent back the other letter . . . the one the folks left me who'd raised me. So she knows it'll be me, all right."

London's brows faintly contracted. "You mean she didn't know she was hiring her own son when she sent for you an' me?"

Bellanger shook his head. "She didn't know, but I did. Y'see, couple of years back I drifted through the Brigham country, askin' questions and chasin' down the leads. I saw her. I saw that ranch, too, and her husband, and the little kids."

London kept staring at Bellanger. "What in hell did you send her the letter for?" he asked. "Why didn't you just join me an' ride down, do your work like we're bein' hired to do, and ride off again?"

Lou eased back, tossed aside his hat, and looked over at Two-Gun Jim London. "I don't know," he murmured. "I honestly don't know, Jim. I've asked myself that a dozen times since I did it. I just plain don't know. Maybe it was to let her know I was comin' to help an' for her not to worry any more . . . I don't know."

Jim London sat up and removed his coat. He then went over and rummaged in a saddlebag and returned to their supper fire with a pony of brandy. "I need it. Maybe you don't, but I sure do. I never rode into one

56

like this before. I just hope it doesn't get so complicated I can't ride out again."

They ate and drank their spiked coffee and sat afterward smoking in long silence. The night dropped in around their hiding place first, then slowly made its gloomy way up the brushy slopes to the higher places. The daytime heat diminished. A big old rodent-hunting horned owl skimmed along, caught the updraft from the fire, and frantically beat its powerful wings to get away from that frightening place.

When the moon arose, lifting perfectly over the hill on their right, London made a pillow of his coat and lay back. He'd come a long way and, even without the bizarre story he'd been told that afternoon, was tired enough to sleep like a rock, which is exactly what he did.

Lou Bellanger sat and smoked and watched the fire until it died down to coals, before he, too, rolled over and slept.

CHAPTER
FOUR

It was still dark when they struck camp. It was also chilly, so each of them put on their coats. Jim London's Prince Albert, rumpled and dusty and travel-stained, still made him look like an undertaker. If he hadn't worn one of those stiff-brimmed, low-crowned hats that was also black, perhaps the illusion wouldn't have been so readily noticeable.

Bellanger, on the other hand, wore the usual cowboy's riding jacket, blanket-lined, and also the usual gray Stetson hat and scuffed boots. Perhaps, except for his tied-down gun with its little hammer tie-down and the obviously reversed leather of the flesh-out holster, Lou could have passed for an average range rider. Still, there were enough significant differences in both men not to fool observant people. In the Brigham country of northern Arizona most people were observant, with or without reason; it did no harm to scrutinize each and every stranger.

Their horses were also different, and yet they had two outward characteristics in common; both were obviously animals of excellent breeding, and both were built to run fast. It was impossible to know in advance when a man might have to shoot first and ride hardest.

58

If he were successful in the first, it did not follow that he'd survive just because he'd shot first; unless, in the second place, he also had the means for outdistancing all pursuit. Well-bred, deep-chested, powerful-legged horses were very expensive. Life insurance never came cheap.

The horses were sure-footed, but Lou knew the land, too, and that helped even with the moon gone and only the stars brightening their way. He didn't speak often as he rode along. He didn't appear particularly alert or preoccupied, just drowsy and chilly. He bore along southwestward, eventually coming down across the cow-country range west of Brigham. He'd purposefully worked closer in than he'd had to. When they could see, he pointed off toward the clutter of squares and angles and blocks, saying: "Brigham."

Two-Gun Jim London looked and nodded and followed along. He didn't say anything. There really wasn't much to say in any case. Brigham was a cow-country town. It followed most of the architectural precedents of other cow towns. Besides, Jim London was both cold and hungry.

They swerved due west and rode for nearly an hour, with a little hint of dawn wetting down the gun-metal eastern horizon, then halted finally atop a low hill that curved slightly like a half moon, from south to north. This was grassland, out here. There were trees scattered handsomely, but there was very little sage or chaparral. At one time no doubt the scrub brush had flourished, but it was gone now except along the lip of gulches or in the shallow depths of erosion cuts. In general, the land lay flat to rolling. A half to three-quarters of a mile ahead stood the dark, clumsy patch of buildings cast down beside a little cottonwood creek in the middle of all this hushed, unending immensity.

"That it?" asked Jim.

"That's it," replied Lou.

"Looks like we got here before breakfast." As soon as Jim said that, though, a yellow sputter of lamplight shone down there. He looked at Bellanger. "Well, do they meet us out here or do we ride on down? Sometimes folks are squeamish. Not very many like having fellers such as you 'n' me riding right up into the dooryard."

Lou urged his horse forward without commenting. They covered the intervening distance and kept watching that lamplight. It was the only warmth in all the moonless predawn.

Lou rode into the dark barn and stepped down to off saddle. Jim wasn't so sure about this and said he thought he'd just leave his horse saddled and tied for the time being. He also said something else, after going back to the doorless front of the barn and looking all around.

"Where's the dog? Lou, these folks got a lot to learn. A two-bit pup's the best way in the world to keep from bein' shot in your sleep."

They crossed to the house and Lou rapped. For ten seconds nothing happened, then a man eased around the far end of the house with a carbine and said: "Which one of you is Bellanger?"

London turned very slowly. Bellanger, also, came around. They stonily regarded the crouched-over rifleman without saying a word. There was something about a pointed gun barrel that took the desire for conversation out of a man, even a man who'd looked into those gun barrels before.

"I ask which one of you is Bellanger," the man said again.

London turned a little tart, saying: "Mister, you better point that carbine some other way. My patience is getting a little thin. If you don't know Bellanger when you see him, what makes you think either one of us is him?"

"Well," grumbled the other man, letting his gun barrel sag a trifle, "he's due here, an' I'd say one of you fellers has to be him."

Lou spoke finally, his voice very soft and slow-running: "What'd you figure to do, mister, shoot Bellanger?"

The rifleman didn't answer. He seemed to be trying to understand something. It was a woman's voice speaking gently that took the man's truculence away. She spoke from inside an open window where there was no light. "Jamie, it's all right. Let the gentlemen in by the front door. Jamie, put the gun down."

The man obeyed. London and Bellanger exchanged a look. They steadily eyed the man as he shuffled forward without looking at either of them again, opened the door and jerked his head for them to step inside. Just before he moved, Jim London said in a low whisper: "Welcome home, Lou."

In the dark it was difficult to tell much about the ranch, but it never was essential to ride over the land of a cow outfit if a man could see the inside of the owner's house. This particular house had several pieces of scuffed furniture in the parlor, a granite fireplace, doors leading into other parts of the house, and very little else. It didn't look quite like the inside of a genuine hard-luck ranch, but neither did it look at all prosperous. The smell of food was strong, too, and coffee, but the only light came from the kitchen. It filtered into the little threadbare parlor through a partially open door making it awkward for the four people in there, who were trying to study one another without enough light to do it by.

It didn't occur to Jim London or Lou Bellanger right away that this was no oversight. The woman purposefully hadn't brought the light into the parlor. She said, looking at the gunfighters from back in shadows: "Jamie is Mister Hudson. You'll have to excuse him. They hurt him badly last fall and he hasn't gotten all his senses back yet . . ." She let her voice dwindle off.

Jim London looked at the man, then back at the woman. She stood straight, but the man seemed oddly bent to the right as though listening to distant voices. Jim said: "I'm London. This is Bellanger." Then he stepped away from beside Lou and said: "Come along, Jamie. Let's you 'n' me get a cup of that coffee." He took Jamie's arm and marched him out into the kitchen. Jamie didn't resist at all; in fact, he seemed somehow pleased to be taken along. When they passed

62

into the orange light, he turned, making a gargoyle smile at the younger man. Jim stopped cold.

Someone had hit Jamie Hudson in the face with what must have been a shovel. His nose had been smashed flat, his lips split, and one eyebrow had a livid red scar that reached above it half across the forehead, and lower down across one cheek. The marks were unmistakably the signs of violence, and they were still shiny red and freshly healed.

Jim went to the stove, poured two cups of coffee, took one back, and said: "Sit down, Jamie." He kept studying the wrecked features, sipping coffee, and hearing low, hesitant voices from the parlor. He finished, pushed the cup away, and said: "Jamie, who worked you over?"

The other man was in his forties. He was graying; there were deep crow's-feet lines around his eyes, and his hands were big-veined from labor. But his glance, when he lifted it to Jim London, was mistily young. Too young.

"It was a misunderstanding," he said, arising. "Like some more coffee?"

"No thanks, I'll wait for breakfast. Jamie, what kind of a misunderstanding?"

"Oh, just some men from Mexican Hat . . ." Hudson shuffled after a refill for his cup. Jim turned, watching. Jamie's hands were as steady as stone and he seemed in all other ways perfectly co-ordinated, except for the adolescent look in his eyes and the slightly twisted, shoulder-forward way he moved. As he resumed his seat, he said: "Mexican Hat is the big cow outfit that adjoins us to the north, east an' west. It's the biggest an' richest cow outfit in all the Brigham country."

London nodded, dropped his gaze, and started making a smoke. Out in the parlor there was silence now. He lit up, carefully put the unlit match in the cuff of his trousers, and said: "What were you goin' to do with that carbine tonight, Jamie?"

The answer came candidly. "Shoot Bellanger."

Jim gazed across the table but showed no change in expression. "Why?" he asked.

"Well. Bellanger shot Bob Nichol, didn't he? Bush-whacked him right out there in the middle of the road, didn't he?"

Jim tilted his head, blew smoke at the ceiling, and said softly: "I'll be damned." He looked down. "I'll be *double* damned." He got up, strode to the parlor door, and said: "Lou, Miz Hudson, daylight'll be along directly. Maybe we ought to have a mite of breakfast and talk."

Across the yard a horse whinnied. At once Jim stepped back beside the table and blew down into the chimney of the lamp, plunging the kitchen into a bluish, steely gloom. Jamie's wife came into the room with Bellanger right behind her. She said: "It's nothing, Mister London. We're just a little slow at doing the chores. The horses should've been fed a while back. They're impatient."

Bellanger resettled the hat atop his head and made for the back door. "I'll take care of that," he murmured, and passed quickly outside. London swept back his coat, hooked it under his shell belt, and stepped past the door frame into the gray predawn. As Bellanger strode straight across the yard, Jim shook his head. But nothing happened.

London went back into the kitchen. Mrs. Hudson hadn't relighted the lamp and she kept her back to Jim over at the stove. Her voice was calm, though; in fact, it seemed weary and too calm.

"I explained to Lou, Mister London. We have water rights to the creek Mexican Hat needs if they are to develop this southern sector of their range. We can't sell them. If we did that, then our range would be worthless. We offered to divide the water, but Mexican Hat's superintendent says his outfit needs all the water. They offered to buy us out. Jamie and I've been working here for eight years, Mister London. We couldn't start over somewhere else for what they offered . . . even if we wanted to leave."

Jim hung his hat upon a wall peg and dropped astraddle a chair. "What happened to Jamie?" he asked, studying the sturdy, short back of the woman over at the stove.

"No one really knows, Mister London. He was out setting posts with the wagon. He was to be gone all day, so I didn't worry. Then the wagon came home and Jamie was in the back. I thought he was dead. Doctor Hart from town said it was a miracle he wasn't dead. That's all anyone knows for certain."

"Yeah," said Jim quietly, examining his empty coffee cup. "Pretty hard for a man to hit himself in the face with a shovel four or five times, Missus Hudson." He found a speck of coffee grounds inside the cup and used a fingernail to remove it. "Tell me, did Jamie ever mention Mexican Hat after it happened?"

"Yes. He has moments when he's very lucid, Mister London. Usually, though, he's . . . well . . . as you've seen him this morning. Childish and so . . . so . . . helpless."

"Sure. Well, what did he say about Mexican Hat? Whose name did he mention?"

"Three men, Mister London. Frank Holden, Bell Forrester, and the Mexican Hat range boss, Ewell Frith." Finally Judith Hudson turned. She was perfectly composed. She said: "Lou explained to me that he's told you I'm his mother, Mister London."

Just for a second a shadow of quick and fleeting embarrassment passed across those gold-flecked eyes, then Jim London stood up as though he hadn't heard a word and trooped over to the stove. "That's mighty good coffee," he said, refilling the cup. "Mighty good. It's been a long time for me . . . for Lou too, I reckon . . . since we had any decent coffee." As he turned slowly back, his cup filled, to gaze upon the woman's lifted face, London said: "Y'know, Miz Hudson, when I got your letter up in Laramie, I told myself this was just another job. That's all, just another job."

Jamie came shuffling back into the kitchen from outside. Lou was with him. Judith Hudson turned suddenly, very busy getting breakfast. Bellanger told London he'd taken the saddle and bridle off Jim's horse, fed and watered it. Then he rolled up his sleeves, hung his hat on a peg, and took the chunk of rough lye soap Jamie handed him and ducked back outside again to wash up.

Over along the top of the eastward land swell lying a half or three-quarters of a mile away, a ribbon of light began to build up steadily. Farther off, the sky turned from gray to blue, and from pink to yellow. Dawn had arrived. The sun hadn't jumped up yet, but it would, very shortly now.

Jim went to a window, swished his coffee, and said: "How much stock do you folks run, Miz Hudson?"

She had her apron up using it as a lifter to hold the hot platter with when she answered from over by the table. "Not much any more. No cattle any more at all, and only the horses we keep corralled or stalled."

"But you did have cattle, didn't you?"

"Yes," she murmured. "At one time we'd built up to sixty-five cows and two grade bulls."

"What happened . . . Mexican Hat?"

"Well, not entirely, Mister London. We still had thirty head left when I wrote you and . . . Mister Bellanger. We sold those to have your . . . wages."

"But Mexican Hat got the others?"

She turned, facing London. "I didn't see them do it. Neither did Jamie. We just don't have the livestock any more."

CHAPTER
FIVE

Because the Hudsons had never hired men, they had no bunkhouse. However, they did have a fair-size harness room just inside their log barn, so Lou and Jim put up over there.

They had a full day to waste. After settling in, they spent the first three hours of it sleeping in bunks they rigged out of scantling timbers and ropes woven back and forth to form springs. Over these ropes they flung their bedrolls. It worked out very well.

By noon they'd had their rest and went down to the creek to wash and shave. And also to talk, for they knew now all they had to know. There were still plenty of loose ends, such as how many toughs rode for this Mexican Hat outfit, and what peril there might be for Lou around the countryside after what had been alleged against him in that Utah newspaper. But primarily these two were calculating, knowledgeable men. They lived with danger and violence from day to day. They had inherent carefulness, but they did not employ any more caution than that.

"Right now," said Jim, shaving with his polished steel mirror propped against a tree trunk, high up, "it looks to me the thing to do is meet Mexican Hat. Now I'd guess an outfit as big as I think this one might be likely has eight or ten steady riders. Ordinarily I'd say we'd go into town and catch the range boss first, then commence whittlin' down from there. But now I'll have to ride in alone."

Lou was finished shaving. "You still got that walnut stain?" he asked, and London looked around.

"Hell, I forgot," he muttered. "Sure, it's in my left saddlebag there on the creekbank. But you got to have hot water to make it look right and stain permanent." He watched Lou walk away, then said: "And you also got to have different clothes."

Lou dug for the bottle, found it, and wordlessly headed for the Hudson house, leaving Jim to finish his shaving alone. When London was done cleaning up, he beat his coat to knock off the heavy layers of dust, then he shook it out and shrugged into it. A small lizard darted up the tree where Jim's steel mirror was and cocked a jaunty eye at the human. Jim looked back, fishing for a comb inside his coat. "You're lucky," he told the little beady-eyed lizard. "All you got to worry about is catching a fly asleep, or maybe findin' a lady lizard." He finished combing, brushed off his black hat, and dropped it onto the back of his head, took down the mirror, and caught up his saddlebag before starting toward the improvised bunkhouse at the barn.

He'd cuffed his horse and wiped off his saddle before Lou returned, his hair darkened to an auburn tint, his skin as dark almost as the hide of the saddle maker in town, and grinning.

In a lilting, mocking, way he said: "*Buenos dias, señor, eet ees a fairy nize day, no?*"

London said: "No. Not with those blue eyes, *chollo*."

Lou was wearing some faded clothing that didn't quite fit but which came close enough. "Jamie's," he said, and the name sobered him. He went after his horse.

They rode out of the yard with the sun gliding down the western sky. They didn't have much to say except for a short period when they discussed Jamie Hudson. It was then that Lou explained about the children. "She's got them living with friends in town. She told me she thought it was safer, since what happened to Jamie."

Jim London nodded. "What happened to Jamie, I reckon, is that someone meant to bash in his skull. But Jamie must have a solid granite head." Jim looked rueful. "Did she tell you if this pill-pusher in Brigham said he'd ever snap out of it, or be like that all the rest of his days?"

"The doctor didn't know. Seems not too much is known about what happens inside a man's head when he's beaten like that."

London started making a cigarette. Lou gazed ahead through the lazy, warm afternoon, watching the town come out to them, and up northward a band of riders was skirting the roadway as though they'd come from some place far to their right. They kicked up quite a gray cloud of dust, which meant there were probably five or six men in the party. Lou said, eyeing those faraway horsemen: "Mexican Hat."

Jim looked as he lit up. "You sure of that?"

"No. But Mexican Hat's nearest cow camp lies beyond the creek north and west of the Hudson place. I reckon it's a fair enough guess."

Lou shot a look at the descending sun. By the time they got to the outskirts of Brigham, another hour or so if they continued just poking along this way, it would be early dusk. He yawned, stretched, and popped a seam in the back of the threadbare old jumper he'd borrowed from Jamie. Jim grinned. "If you do that to the britches, we might get locked up for indecent exposure. By the way, you got any ideas?"

"None at all," replied Bellanger. "They don't know you, so there's no problem there. Me, I'll split off from you an' sort of circulate around. If I see any Mexican Hatters, you'll know about it."

London said: "*Humph!* How many did she say they had ridin' for this outfit? Eight or ten, or something like that? Then we better map out something, Lou, because those are pretty powerful odds in any man's language."

Bellanger drifted along, gazing ahead at the town. He seemed neither impressed by what London had just said nor particularly concerned with what lay ahead for him, either. "I been thinking," he murmured. "Why does a woman deserve something like this? Hell, she was an orphan. Then there was this big handsome bronc' rider who came along. Well, the result of that was me. Then James Hudson, an honest feller willin' to sweat, so she pulled right beside him in double harness. And because of a lousy little creek of water not worth a damn, she gets Jamie back in his wagon, instead of

James. Her two kids livin' in town on bounty, and Jamie makes a third kid for her. Jim, what makes things turn out like that for some folks and not for others?"

London, the practical man, said simply: "Who knows? All a feller can do in this life, Lou, is get through the best way he can, and don't wonder too much about the why and how of things. Now about this Mexican Hat outfit. We want three men, Bell Forrester, Frank Holden, and the range boss, a feller named Ewell Frith. That'll square the books for Jamie. After that . . ."

"Wait a minute, Jim. How will that square the books for Jamie? Hell, Jamie's all right. Most of the time he's as happy as a ten-year-old kid. *He* doesn't know. It's *her* that's got to be squared up for. An' how do you do that? I can take care of this Frith an' Holden and Forrester. But that doesn't end it, Jim."

London smashed his smoke atop the saddle horn, looking acidly harsh. But he rode 100 yards before speaking. Then his voice was thin-edged but under perfect control. "Get something through your head, Lou. Fellers like us can only do one thing . . . even the score. We can't make life over, nor go ridin' around playin' Robin Hood. You get an eye for an eye, then you get the hell out of the country before an army of clodhoppers or lynch-happy cowboys catches you." Jim squinted at the town. They could hear sounds now, boys hooting back and forth, dogs barking, somewhere a heavy-bagged milk cow complaining that her milker was late at his chores, a woman yelling in falsetto exasperation at her children. "I know, you're personally tied into all this. It's no good, Lou. When a man in our trade does that, he's askin' for it. Nine times out of ten he'll get it, too. Now, listen, I'll split off an' head up toward the saloon with the most horses at the tie rack, if there's more'n one bar to this place. I'll try and pick up what I can about Mexican Hat. You find the livery barn and hang around out front down there . . . in the shadows. We got to find 'em fast, call 'em fast, an' shoot fast. That's all. It's just in a day's work."

Bellanger still seemed not to be listening, but eventually he peeled off to the right when the outlying sheds and houses of Brigham loomed ahead. London watched him go, shook his head, and told his horse for the second or third time he'd never gotten tangled up in a job like this one before, and it made him a little uneasy having an emotional friend involved with him.

"It's a hell of a lot better all round just to ride in, pick 'em out before the whole blessed countryside knows trouble's arrived, force a fight, and get it over with, then get to hell on down the pike."

London passed over a vacant plot between two stores and his horse jumped, clearing the front roadway plank walk handily. Across the road several riders were baying at the moon — or stars — out front of the Trail Saloon, smoked to the gills and being encouraged at this odd sport by a half dozen other laughing range riders. London tied up at the crowded rack, but only with a single loop over the pole instead of a knot, and walked on over. It was shadowy over there. He paused on the plank walk to turn a slow look down the roadway at places where lamps were being lighted here and there. Out front of the livery barn several patient horses drooped, unsaddled except for one leggy beast with a man slouched down upon a bench at the horse's head. As Jim London watched, an old man shuffled past that slouched figure down there, paused, turned back, and said something. The slouched figure looked up. For a moment those two spoke together, then the slouched figure straightened a little, and motioned for the old man to sit upon the bench beside him. London stood a moment considering that affair down there. In the end he decided that Lou would know exactly what to do, regardless, and turned to walk casually over and enter the saloon, out front of which those cowboys were still hilariously egging on their pair of drunken friends in their obvious competition to see which one could best simulate a coyote while baying at the purple heavens.

The Trail was crowded. It was Friday night, not Saturday, but judging from the size of the restless crowd a lot of riders must have misjudged or lost a day somewhere, and were in town to celebrate Saturday night. It happened like that often enough; men who worked according to the sun and stars could very easily lose track of days. Sometimes it was even easy to lose track of a whole month.

Elmer was tending the bar, but he looked dour about it. Jim London couldn't have known that Elmer was the day barman, not the night man. Neither could he have known the night man was ill, therefore Elmer had to assume both shifts, which accounted for his gritty expression.

All Jim thought, gazing at Elmer, was that this barman was a cantankerous cuss, which seems to be the way most first impressions are established, not with justification, but out of full ignorance. Elmer wasn't cantankerous at all; he was worrisome and intent and sometimes too prying with his curiosity, but he wasn't disagreeable. At least he wasn't normally.

Two weathered cowmen leaning elbow to elbow beside Jim London were discussing the condition of Sheriff Bob Nichol. One said: "You'd think, if he was goin' to die, he'd do it, instead of squeakin' along a breath at a time."

The other one was less callous. "I figure for every day he pulls through, he's that much closer to makin' a full recovery."

The first cowman drained his glass, shoved it out, and raised a finger to Elmer as he said, somewhat sardonically: "Well. That's not always how it works out. Now you take James Hudson, for example."

"Different," muttered the second man, dropping his voice and looking quickly into the backbar mirror at the men on both sides. "A bullet usually does the trick. You either go down an' stay down, or you're up an' around within a day or two. But Hudson got it different. I heard it said he'll never come back from the beatin' he got."

Their drinks came and the man who'd spoken last seemed reluctant, when his companion started giving his opinion of the Hudson matter, to pursue it any further.

Jim had his drink and studied the faces up and down the bar. They were nearly all range men, riders or owners. A few sleeve-gartered townsmen were in the saloon, but not many. The difficulty for Jim London was the same old difficulty. A stranger in a strange town had to determine which were the men he wanted. Asking questions of bartenders usually was poor policy. Bartenders frequently smelled trouble and slipped a warning down the line.

Jim turned, hooking both elbows over the bar, and made his leisurely survey of the room. If a man listened long enough, he'd hear a name sometimes, or he'd see a belt buckle with a brand on it, or he'd see a familiar face. This time, it didn't happen in any of those ways. This time a heavy-set, solid cowboy backed into one of Jim's elbows and grunted from the sharpness. He spilled half his drink.

Jim withdrew the offending arm and turned. The cowboy was swearing and slapping whiskey off his front. Then the cowboy turned. He was a few inches shorter than Jim London, but nearly twice as broad and burly. "Mister," he said, resentful and somewhat drunk, "how'd you like to pay for that drink you made me spill?"

Jim nodded without smiling. There were other range men down the bar looking up at him. "Sure," he said, and turned to flag for another drink. The burly man stepped fully around to run a slow look up and down London. His neck was dark red and his fat lips were compressed.

"Mister, how'd you like to buy drinks for the house?" he said, twisting up his lips into a tough and scornful expression.

"Don't have that much money," retorted London, and one of the other cowboys said: "Come on, Bell, cut it out. He said he'd replace the drink you spilt."

"I spilt!" exclaimed Bell Forrester. "I spilt. Dog-gone it, this tinhorn here bumped me on purpose. Jabbed me in the ribs with his cussed bony elbow."

Farther down the bar a tall, hard-faced, older man straightened up, looking past Forrester, taking Jim London's measure. This man said nothing, though. One of the other riders, a scarred and calm-eyed man, said: "Take the drink he'll pay for an' leave it be, Bell."

Jim saw the growing thought of violence in Bell's face and loosened his shoulders as he eased off a little from the bar. Elmer brought Bell's fresh drink. Elmer had heard the loudness down the bar and was looking a little anxious, as though he knew what it meant when Bell Forrester got both loud and half drunk. "Hey," he said leaning to touch Bell's arm, "I'll get another one, on the house."

But Bell wasn't going to be placated. "You go to hell," he told Elmer, glaring. Then he turned. "And you, dude," he said to Jim London. "You step outside."

Jim smiled easily. "Wait a minute," he replied softly. "I said I'd buy the drink."

Bell swung clumsily, but London made no move to duck. The blow caught Jim across the lower cheek, knocking his hat off. Bell followed that up with a string of fighting names. "Now, you yellow-bellied louse, will you step outside?"

Jim stooped to retrieve his hat. He looked impassively at the other cowboys. They in turn were

77

looking at him — some were embarrassed, some looked pained. One or two looked down into their glasses.

Forrester swore some more and started for the roadside door. Everyone in that crowded room was suddenly still and silent. Jim London dusted off his hat, shrugged apologetically at Elmer, and started out of the saloon, too. Behind him Elmer said: "Frank, you 'n' Ewell got to stop this. He's pushin' that stranger into it an' there ain't no reason at all except he's a damned bully when he's been drinkin'."

No one answered, but everyone started gravely trooping out into the night.

CHAPTER
SIX

Jim London was a sharp-witted and observant man. He'd identified all the three names in the back of his mind with faces. Bell Forrester, he would now kill. That hard-looking, taciturn older man, raw-boned, big, and ham-handed, was Ewell Frith, range boss for Mexican Hat, and the rider who'd tried to persuade Bell Forrester to leave it be inside the saloon was Frank Holden.

But Jim had too big an audience. At least two dozen range men pushed out and lined up and down the plank walk, looking out into the roadway where Bell Forrester was taking his wide stance and peering around for Jim London. He was going to have to be satisfied with downing just Forrester, this time.

"Hey, dude!" called Bell. "Come on. What's the matter, you got yellow up your back?"

Jim turned toward the man he knew was Ewell Frith. "Might be better if you'd calm him down," he murmured, meeting Frith's steady, smoky gaze. "He's half drunk."

"So he is," acknowledged the range boss, studying Jim London. "Nothing I can do, mister." Frith's craggy features were expressionless and coldly unemotional.

"If you want, you can go back inside, on through behind the bar, an' out the back way."

Jim eyed Frith a quiet moment, then shrugged and stepped down into the roadway. He was deliberately projecting an impression of total reluctance. As he walked down through the dust southward of where Bell was standing in the center of the star-lighted, empty roadway, he said: "Cowboy, it was a pure accident. If it'll help, I'll stand you all the drinks you want."

Bell swore at London. Over on the plank walk a townsman made a reproachful clucking sound. Bell turned on him in a flash. "You shut up," he snarled, not able to discern who, exactly, had made that noise.

Jim eased back his coat as he paced along, got it securely in behind his gun belt, flicked off the little tie down, and gently loosened the gun in its holster, all before he finally stopped and turned.

They were 200 feet apart. From farther back someone's boots pounding over the wooden sidewalk made the only sound as a belated spectator hurried forward to see this fight.

For four or five seconds the tension mounted, drew out razor-thin, then Bell's right shoulder dropped. London shot him square and hard. Bell's gun was only half out of the holster when he looked up, round-eyed, and coughed. Then he fell in a disheveled heap without moving again. Over on the plank walk two dozen eyes turned in shock toward Jim London, who waited a moment to be certain Bell wouldn't move, before he shucked out the spent casing, plucked a fresh load from

80

his belt, and pushed it home in the cylinder, holstered his gun, and walked to the side.

Ewell Frith was watching London. He was the only man who didn't rush forward, finally, to inspect the corpse. He kept staring until he finally turned on one toe and stalked back inside.

Men came from all directions. Someone had a hand lantern which he lowered after others had spread Bell Forrester out, face up. The bullet hole was no more than a little purple pucker in the dead center of Bell's shirt.

"Through the heart," someone murmured in quiet awe because the light had been very poor.

Jim watched the man he thought was Frank Holden bend to grab hold of the dead man. "I'm sorry," he told Holden, who was a dark curly-haired man with coarse lips and brown eyes. "I sure didn't want to do it. I'll stand the cost of planting him."

Holden briefly gazed at London, then looked away, saying gruffly: "Some of you boys give me a hand. We'll haul him over to Hart's place."

Jim didn't go back into the Trail. He made a smoke to have something to do, lit it, and turned slowly to look southward, down toward the livery barn. Lou's horse was still down there, but Lou wasn't. Jim turned to gaze at the store fronts, the recessed doorways, the little dark passageways between the nearest buildings. He didn't find Lou in any of those places.

A little knot of range men gathered out front of the saloon, speaking in low tones, and from time to time glancing down where Two-Gun Jim London stood.

They'd gotten the body hauled away, too. Across the road three townsmen were also talking among themselves. One of them was a paunchy large man with an ornate gold watch chain strung across his big gut. It was this man who eventually detached himself from his friends and hiked straight over toward Jim. His friends headed for the saloon, evidently to get more of the details of what had happened.

The paunchy man was open-faced and forward acting when he stopped in front of London and said: "My name's Merritt Burgess. I'm chairman of the Brigham town council. I'm sorry about what just happened, but, the way it was said, that Mexican Hat rider forced you into it."

Jim's gold-flecked light brown eyes were curious about this heavy-set man in front of him. "I'm sorry, too," he murmured, weighing and measuring Burgess and coming to several definite conclusions. "It wasn't my doing, an', if I'd known it might happen, I'd have avoided it."

"Mind telling me your name?" Burgess asked.

"No. It's . . . Jim Landon."

"Well, Mister Landon, I own the mercantile business here in Brigham, along with bein' on the council, an' I was just speaking with some of the other councilmen. We have a problem. Some time back a bushwhacker shot down our sheriff. He isn't dead, but chances are he won't be able to be back on the job for maybe four or five months, if then. So, we were wondering, seeing that you can handle yourself right well and all, if you'd be interested in the job. It pays sixty a month and care for one horse at the livery barn, plus ammunition expenses and travelin' funds if you have to take to the trail."

Jim took a long drag of his smoke and gazed straight into Merritt Burgess's eyes without blinking or even seeming to breathe for several long seconds, then he flipped the cigarette away and very thinly smiled as though he were having difficulty from breaking forth into laughter. Finally he said: "Mister Burgess, you don't even know me. As for handling myself, that Mexican Hat cowboy was half drunk."

"All the same, Mister Landon, I was told you did everything possible to avoid it, but when it had to be done, you knew exactly how to do it. Now that's precisely what we need in a sheriff. Listen, if you'll consider it, I'll go see if the other councilmen will raise that ante to seventy-five a month."

Jim gazed down toward the livery barn. Bellanger's horse was gone. He turned back and said: "Let me think it over, Mister Burgess. Let me sleep on it. If I decide to take the job, I'll hunt you up in the morning."

Burgess seemed doubtful, but he said: "That's my store behind you southward. I'll be in the office all morning, Mister Landon. I'll talk to the other councilmen tonight and have the answer for you in the morning on more pay. Good night."

"Yeah," murmured Jim. "Good night."

He stood a full ten minutes, watching Merritt Burgess walk northward up beyond the Trail to the farthest intersection, and turn there to pass westerly down some side road out of sight, then he glanced down in front of the livery barn again and finally walked over to get his horse. He had the animal freed, was turning it away from the rack when hard-eyed, stone-faced Ewell Frith walked out of the saloon's overhang shadows and said: "Mister . . ."

Jim turned, feeling the roughness behind that one word. Frith walked on up. He was just as tall as Jim London and somewhat heavier through the chest and shoulders. His expression was exactly as it had been earlier, when Jim had suggested that he take charge of Bell Forrester and stop the fight — it was darkly weathered and totally impassive, as though Ewell Frith, Mexican Hat's superintendent, either had no feelings at all, or else kept them hidden deep down where they never influenced the look in his eyes or across his tough, rugged face.

"Mister, if I was you, I'd keep on riding, once you get clear of Brigham."

Jim's light brown eyes returned Frith's cold look. "But you're not me," he said softly. "Anything else?"

"Not much," said Frith, studying Jim. "You worked that right well. You knew from the start you could kill him. He didn't hit you in the face in there because he was faster. He hit you because you let him do it, let him make it look like he was forcing the fight."

"He did force it."

"Naw," growled the cold-eyed, older man. "You an' I know a damned sight better. You killed him before he even got his lousy gun out. Mister, a man with that kind of co-ordination could have ducked that slap in the face, easy."

84

Jim raised his boot and toed into the stirrup. He rose up, settled across leather, and checked up his horse as he and Ewell Frith looked straight at one another. "You got pretty good eyesight, Frith," London said. "If it gets any better, maybe you're the one who'll figure he'd better head out for new pastures."

Jim reined away leaving Mexican Hat's rough range boss standing back there in the roadway, gazing after him. Frith's dark brows dropped and his lips pursed in deep thought. He'd been warned about something, he knew that, but he couldn't figure out why. To Ewell Frith's knowledge he'd never before set eyes upon the stranger in the Prince Albert coat. He turned and went ambling back toward the saloon.

Jim left town riding north, but he at once cut back southward down the west side and rode along with his hat tipped back, whistling "Shenandoah". For a mile he got no response. Eventually, when he heard his answering tune, Jim veered off straight westward and kept going until he could skyline the motionless horseman out there on the smooth, night-shadowed plain.

"Which one was it?" Lou asked, before Jim had hardly drawn rein.

"Bell Forrester." Jim then told how he'd let Forrester carry the initiative right up until it came time to shoot. Then, as they leisurely headed back toward the Hudson place, Jim also told him about Merritt Burgess, and his offer of the sheriff's job.

Lou was shocked. "I got in behind a building," he said. "I saw some feller fat as a foaling mare go up and talk to you."

"That was this Burgess feller."

"Well, hell," muttered Bellanger. "Now what?"

London smiled, showing strong white teeth. "I don't know. I know Frith by sight and the other one, the rider named Frank Holden. But Frith told me he thinks I deliberately gunned down Forrester. And this Frith is dangerous, Lou. He's no idiot." Jim paused and gazed at his partner, then asked a question: "Who was the old duffer who sat down on the bench with you, out front of the livery barn?"

Lou grimaced. "You'd never believe it. Here we are, hundreds of miles from the Mex border, and who gets taken in by this walnut stain but an old Mex feller who makes saddles and harness in Brigham. I had to sweat like the devil tryin' to keep up the pretence. This old man's name was Sam Chavez."

But the Chavez interlude got lost as they discussed that matter of replacing Sheriff Bob Nichol. It amused Jim London. "I told Burgess I'd think it over. I also told him my name was Jim Landon. He's going to try and get the town council to raise the pay to seventy-five dollars a month."

"How the hell can you even think of taking it?" demanded Lou. "You said yourself . . . don't get too involved. Ride in, do the job, and ride out fast."

London nearly smiled. "That's the damndest thing I ever had happen to me. Never before have I come close to being offered a badge."

"You're talkin' like a kid," growled Lou.

London turned those odd eyes of his. "Am I, Lou? No one has a better right to go anywhere, any time,

86

than a badge-packin' lawman. I could pick out Frith and Holden one at a time just like that."

Lou hadn't evidently envisaged such latitude because after that he rode along through the chilly night without saying another word until they were almost back to the Hudson place again. Then all he said was: "That's just right, now that I think about it. You could set those two up within twenty-four hours."

Jim London rode the balance of the distance in good spirits. He was whistling "Shenandoah" when they passed down into the darkened yard, but stopped whistling when Lou growled that he'd wake up the Hudsons.

They put up their animals, lit a candle in their improvised bunkhouse, and wordlessly bedded down. It had been a very productive night. Very productive.

CHAPTER
SEVEN

What happened the following day no one anticipated. Probably no one could have anticipated it, even though at least one man who was involved knew how both factions were aligned.

Jim London wasn't that man. Jim left the Hudson place right after breakfast to ride back into Brigham and accept that sheriff's position. Neither he nor Lou Bellanger commented at all about events in town the previous night, and undoubtedly that also had much to do with what happened later in the day.

Mrs. Hudson had Jamie out hoeing weeds in their garden patch behind the house. She came down to the barn to see whether Lou and Jim had any laundry they wanted cleaned and ironed. Lou had some, but he lied about it; he'd been doing his own washing so long it no longer was a chore. He'd go right on doing it himself, and told Mrs. Hudson that.

It was a cheerful springtime morning, clear as glass in all directions, golden-warm and fragrant. Judith Hudson lingered down by the barn where Lou was soaping his saddle and bridle in the dooryard. She didn't say much although she left the clear impression there was a lot dammed up inside her she'd have let loose, if only she'd known how.

Lou smoked and vigorously rubbed, in the identical mood of dumb-brute awkwardness, so they were close together down there in the fragrant warmth, quiet and uncomfortable. Finally she said — "I'd better go after the eggs." — and moved away toward the henhouse.

He stopped rubbing leather, looked after her gravely, then returned to his work. When he was finished, for lack of anything better to do, he also cleaned and oiled his six-gun, then brought forth the Hudsons' team harness and went to work on that. It was near noon by this time, with a soft little groundswell of air stirring the grass and bringing to the ranch yard a wonderful stillness.

Jamie came ambling over to sit upon a nail keg with the hoe between his knees amiably to converse. For a while Jamie was easy and relaxed at it. For that same little while Lou humored him. Then Jamie gradually changed, even his voice deepened and roughened and became more positive as he said: "I don't like to see this happen, Bellanger. I know who you are, of course. Your mother showed me the letter you sent back to her when she wrote up to Vernal to hire you for this job. I wish it could've been any other gunfighter, Bellanger. Any other gunfighter at all. It was bad enough for her to learn that you were a gunfighter. It'd be worse, if bringin' you down here to help us got you killed. Bellanger, have you any idea what a thing like this can do to a sensitive woman like your mother?"

Lou leaned on the tie rack where he had the harness strung out and gazed straight at Jamie. This was obviously one of Jamie's lucid moments. "Sure, I have an idea what findin' out her son was a gunfighter . . . and maybe worse . . . would do to any woman. But, Jamie, I came of my own free will. You see, I knew who she was long before she knew who I was. So I didn't have to come at all, except that I wanted to."

"Why, Bellanger? You haven't even seen her in twenty years."

"Maybe that was why, Jamie. Or maybe because a man's got leanings toward his kinfolk. Hell, I understood a long time ago why she had to put me out with the folks who raised me. If you're figurin' I resented that, or hated her for it, you're all wrong, Jamie. She was just a kid herself. You know that?"

Jamie nodded and stared a moment at the ground, saying nothing, his battered, scarred face loosening, turning sad and anxious and baffled.

Lou said: "Listen, Jamie, you 'n' Miz Hudson had to send your own kids into town in case Mexican Hat hit the ranch. Well, suppose that happened and someone got bad hurt. The folks in town would end up raisin' your kids. You understand what I'm saying?"

"I understand," Jamie muttered, and looked up. "But, boy, I hate something like this. No one wins and folks get to hating so hard they lose sight of what's worthwhile in life. The decent things, you know."

"Sure I know. But what's the alternative, Jamie? Handing the ranch over to Mexican Hat, takin' their couple of hundred dollars, and moving on?"

Jamie shook his head morosely. "No, because I'm too old to start all over again. Lou, I'm forty-nine years old. You understand? That's 'way too old to even try findin' another decent piece of land. And a man needs the respect o' his children. They'd know in a few years . . . they're too young now . . . but in a few years they'd understand that their pa was a coward."

Lou went to work making a cigarette. It was during this quiet interval that he heard the riders coming and whirled to look out over the range without bothering to complete his smoke. "Go on over to the house," he said sharply. "Jamie, get inside an' stay in there. Take Miz Hudson inside with you. Go on, move!"

Jamie jumped up and started swiftly away, carrying the hoe with him. He didn't even pause to look around the northwest corner of his own barn to see who those horsemen were. He simply jumped up and went agitatedly hustling away.

Lou left the harness on the rack out front of the barn, stepped into the shadowy gloom heading toward the improvised bunkhouse, caught up his Winchester from its saddle boot, and stepped rapidly to the rear of the barn where he could see without being seen.

The easiest man to recognize among those oncoming riders was the raw-boned, resolute, sun-bronzed man out front: Ewell Frith, range boss of Mexican Hat.

Lou looked at the others with Ewell Frith. There were four of them, hard-faced, rough men, capable and confident and riding with the slouched posture of unfeeling men who knew exactly what they were riding into, and knew exactly how they'd handle it.

Frith led his men closer to the barn, then on around into the yard, making it appear almost as though he'd jumped up out of the earth, if anyone was watching from the main house. And, of course, someone would be watching. A terrified, wan little woman in her late middle years, and a scarcely rational man who'd survived a savage beating it hadn't been considered he could have survived.

Frith slowed his mount to a walk and led off up through the yard past the barn's doorless dark opening, over to the rickety tie rack out front of the main house. There he stopped, sat like an Indian for a long time without dismounting or calling out, and balefully regarded the hushed and weathered little house.

"Come out!" he eventually called, his voice a rolling growl of harshness in the beautiful, golden day. "You Hudsons, come out. I got something to tell you."

Lou was on the north side of the barn doorway, farthest away. He was standing in speckled shade looking straight up at the backs of those five mounted men where he could also see the skimpy little front porch under its wooden awning. When Jamie's wife came outside with both hands clasped together in the folds of her apron, Lou could see all the agony and fear in her even from the considerable distance separating them. He cocked his Winchester, then uncocked it, set it against the wall close by, and drew his handgun. For this kind of shooting the range was about right, and what he'd need wouldn't be rifle accuracy so much as handgun speed. He stepped just over the threshold where dazzling daylight struck, and called ahead.

"Frith! Turn around!"

Those words hit Mexican Hat's riders in the back, hard. There was no mistaking the tone or the lethal meaning in them. One cowboy swung his head but the others stiffened in their saddles, caught flat-footed, and momentarily confused.

"I said turn around, Frith. The rest of you sit as you are."

Frith put a hand aft of the cantle, twisting from the waist. He gazed straight at Lou and didn't bat an eye. "Well, well," he growled skeptically, "Bellanger. Dyed your hair and hide but I've seen wanted pictures of you. So you didn't leave the country, after all. Bellanger, that was just plain dumb, shooting Bob Nichol. If you try shooting me, it'll be even more stupid. You figure you can shoot all five of us?"

"I've got six bullets, Frith," answered Lou. "That'd leave me one to spare. Unless you want two slugs instead of one."

Frith laughed. It was a steely, bitter sound. "No matter how good you are, Bellanger, you're not *that* good. Five to one. You'd never get it done. This time it wouldn't be like ambushin' Bob Nichol. We'd fight back."

"All right," said Lou. "Any time you're ready, range boss."

But Frith still leaned loosely, gazing back. He obviously wasn't going to force this fight. His riders were like statues, realizing perfectly that any wrong move now could send bullets tearing into their backs.

"What brought you over here, Frith?" Lou asked. "And for once in your lousy life, tell the truth."

"I don't have to lie to people like these," growled the older man. "What brought me over here? An order for the Hudsons to evacuate, to get off this land."

"Just like that?" asked Lou.

"Yeah. Just like that. Unless o' course they'd prefer to stay and . . ." Frith lifted his shoulders, then dropped them. "Let's just say it'll sure be a sight better for us all if they move on. I've got five hundred dollars in an envelope inside my jacket. I've also got a quitclaim for 'em to sign. Then we'll even help 'em load their furniture an' hitch up their wagon. That's why I brought these men along. To help out."

Lou's eyes were very pale in the russet frame of his face. He was briefly silent. When next he spoke, his voice had changed completely. It was soft and just a little slurred. "I reckon I'll put you out of business," he said, and fired.

Frith hadn't been expecting that. Even when the bullet hit him, wrenching him upright and violently sideward, he looked more astonished than hostile.

The gunshot, though, was the spring release. Those four other mounted men, convinced they were to be shot down in cold blood, threw themselves this way and that. Two hit the ground clawing for their handguns. The other two dropped low across the off side of their animals and dug in the spurs. Lou didn't pay much attention to these two; he consistently fired at the two on the ground, moving sideways all the time he was in action. Once, one of the mounted men tried a wild shot

94

from beneath the neck of his plunging horse, but the other cowboy just hung on for dear life and mercilessly rowelled his mount to get out of gun range as rapidly as possible.

The entire battle didn't last three full minutes. As a matter of fact, from the first shot to the last shot, it probably didn't last a total of sixty seconds. But it was still close to three full minutes before the final echoes died out and the three men sprawling there in the golden sunlight were helpless, groaning and cursing, wallowing in powdery dust.

Jamie was over on the porch with his wife. She was clinging to him. Jamie had that old carbine again, but it wasn't even cocked. He was lunging one way and another, making deep-down animal sounds in his throat.

Lou stood in the rank smoke, waiting and watching. Finally he said: "Miz Hudson, take Jamie in the house. You hear me, Jamie? Go on in the house and put up that carbine."

It took a little time. Jamie's agitation couldn't be turned on and off so easily, but with the noise and violence ended, he eventually permitted himself to be herded back inside.

Lou remained where he was long enough to reload, then he paced on across, six-gun holstered, and said to Ewell Frith: "Stand up. You're only hit in the shoulder. Stand up on your damned feet!" He went to the other two. One of those had a broken leg; that one he left sitting where he was, clinging with both hands to the red-splattered leg. The next man was hit high and to one side, in the body. He also told that one to stand. He kicked their guns away, picked up their hats, and crushed them on each man's head.

"Frith, it's your left shoulder. That was on purpose. I'll get your pistol and arm you with it. Would you like an even break right here?"

Frith wasn't in as much pain as shock. He didn't reply; he didn't even seem to understand clearly. The other one with the body shot said through clenched teeth: "Leave him be, Bellanger. Look at his eyes. He doesn't even know where he is."

Lou turned on this one. The cowboy was gingerly stuffing a handkerchief beneath his soggy shirt. "What's your name?" he asked.

"Holden. Frank Holden."

Bellanger digested that, eyeing Holden thoughtfully. "Pretty handy with a shovel, Holden? Pretty handy, you 'n' Forrester and Frith, catching a man working on his fence and trying to beat his brains out with his own shovel?"

The man on the ground gasped out. "Damn it, one of you fellers give me a belt to tie this thing off with. The blood's spurtin' straight up."

Holden looked past Bellanger, then walked over to kneel and help the man with the broken leg. He kept his back to Lou and didn't say a word all the while he made the tourniquet.

Lou caught their horses, led them back, and, when Holden finished and stood up, he handed him the reins. Ewell Frith was beginning to recover from shock and feel the searing pain. Lou jerked his head at Frith.

"Get on your horse. Holden, help your friend up, too. Frith, you listen to me. I could've cut you three down and likely got at least one of the others, too, if I'd aimed to kill. This was a warning."

Frith said: "You set yourself up, Bellanger. You set yourself up for the whole . . ."

"Shut up and listen," snarled Bellanger. "The Hudsons had sixty-five cows and two bulls. They also had some horses. You've got ten days to find 'em, or replace 'em. That's why I didn't kill you. Ten days to make good. After that, I'm comin' for you, bad shoulder or no bad shoulder, and next time I figure to kill you. As for the creek and the land, you tell whoever's your boss at Mexican Hat, just one more visit over here by Mexican Hat, and I'll come after him, too. Now mount up and get the hell out of here."

Holden helped the other cowboy aboard and mounted up himself. He didn't offer Ewell Frith a hand, but Frith made it because Lou Bellanger gave him a rough boost. Then the three of them turned their walking horses and started riding. It wasn't quite high noon.

CHAPTER
EIGHT

Jim didn't return to the ranch until after nightfall, and he came in from the west, which was completely out of his way since he'd ridden from town. Lou was in the barn without any light and heard the horse approaching long before he slipped outside to make certain it was Jim London.

Jim rode inside the barn before dismounting. He said gruffly: "No light. I can't stay anyway. Lou, why the hell didn't you kill them both? I told you . . . this playin' Robin Hood's no good. If you'd killed Holden and Frith, I'd have made a posse, led it in the opposite direction, lost 'em somewhere, and ridden on back to join up with you."

"Not in the back," stated Lou. "That's how it happened. They were over in front of the house."

"Hell, that's no excuse. All you had to do was call them."

Jim dismounted, stepped to the head of his mount where he could clearly see Lou's face in the moonlight, and looked exasperated. "Three bigwigs from Mexican Hat came into town loaded for bear. They brought those wounded men in a wagon for the doctor to patch up. The whole blessed town's in an uproar. It couldn't have been any worse if you'd killed those men, and, as far as I'm concerned, I wish you had. Now, it's all got to be started over again. On top of that, I got to go ridin' all over the lousy countryside tryin' to pick up your sign with a posse of local yokels, and I just don't like riding that much. Not when it's for something as silly and useless as this."

Lou listened and looked at London, and almost smiled. Jim wasn't angry; he was exasperated. He wore the sheriff's badge on his coat and that seemed even more ludicrous. "Frith knew me," he told Jim. "The dye didn't work."

"The dye worked," grunted Jim London. "All it's supposed to do is prevent detection. It's not supposed to hide you completely when you jump out in broad daylight and throw down on five men, Lou. Don't blame it on the dye. And I had one hell of a time keeping half the cowboys and townsmen in the country from riding out here this afternoon, too."

Lou wasn't too concerned with that. He said: "I figured on riding out, then I got to remembering there were more Mexican Hat riders, and figured I'd better lie close in case they came whooping over here to square up for Frith and those other damned fools."

"No one bothers the Hudsons," said Jim. "I laid down that law to Mexican Hat. Anyone else comes over here without bein' invited, I'm going after him personally."

"How did Mexican Hat like that?"

"They didn't, Lou, and I don't give a damn. I told them if they want to see the Hudsons after this, mail 'em a letter or come to me, an' I'll ride out with whatever it is they want said."

"They won't do it!" exclaimed Lou. "Did they tell you what Frith was doing over here?"

"Lookin' for strays."

"That's a lousy lie, Jim. Frith said he had five hundred dollars and a quitclaim deed. He also said if the Hudsons didn't sign it . . ."

London nodded. "I believe you," he said, not waiting for Lou to finish, if indeed Lou had ever meant to finish the sentence. "Now I've got to get back. Lou, don't be anywhere around tomorrow. I'll have to make a big sashay over the countryside with a posse. I'll have to come out here, too, and ask the Hudsons how they come to be harboring a wanted man. They've put up a three hundred dollar bounty on you in Brigham for shooting their sheriff."

"I'll disappear tomorrow," agreed Lou. "But I didn't shoot that tinhorn sheriff."

Jim shrugged. He patently didn't much care who'd shot Bob Nichol. He stepped back beside his horse and lifted his left leg. Just beyond the barn's dark opening a man softly cleared his throat. It wasn't a spontaneous cough or a choke or something that couldn't have been avoided. It was simply the quiet, little, deliberate sound a man makes who seems to wish to announce his presence discreetly.

Jim eased his foot back down and swept back his coat. Lou Bellanger backed off, into the darker shadows, and drew his .45. "That you, Jamie?" he softly called.

"No," came back the muffled reply. "It's Sam Chavez, the saddle maker from town. May I come inside the barn?"

Jim London answered, his voice hardening. "Come right in, Mister Chavez." Jim eased up beside his horse's head, and kept his right hand lightly upon his hip. Lou also eased up a little, the better to catch sight of the saddle and harness maker. Both of them were too astonished, too perplexed, and, at the same time, suspicious to say anything, even after they recognized the old chocolate-colored shuffling figure that stepped diffidently in out of the bland night.

Chavez looked at Lou and smiled. He looked at Jim London and made a slight gesture of deprecation. "I followed you. It's not a nice thing to do, I know."

"Nor healthy," murmured London, eyeing the older man coldly. "Lou, is this the feller who sat on the bench with you down at the livery barn last night?"

Lou said that it was. He also said: "Sam, I didn't do a very good job of fooling you last night, did I?"

The saddle maker made a little gesture. "Well, you did a fair job of it, Mister Bellanger. The trouble is there are so many pictures of you . . ." Sam Chavez smiled that apologetic smile again. Then he turned toward Jim London. "I followed you, Sheriff, not because I expected to find you here . . . like this . . . but to tell you something I didn't want to speak of around town where I'd be seen talking with you."

"Wait a minute," growled London. "How long were you standin' outside the barn tonight, listening?"

101

"I heard what you two said about Sheriff Nichol . . . and . . . other things." Chavez gave his round shoulders a little shrug. "I heard enough. Why should I lie?"

"To stay alive," muttered London, looking brightly and coldly at the saddle maker.

"Wait a minute," Lou broke in. "What is it you wanted to tell the sheriff, Sam?"

"I think I know who shot Sheriff Nichol."

It stunned both Chavez's listeners. This was the first time anyone had said Lou Bellanger hadn't bushwhacked Nichol. Perhaps there were other people who didn't think Bellanger had done it, but this was the first time anyone had had the courage to say it out loud.

London sighed and leaned on his horse, gazing at the older man. "That's what you didn't want to mention in town?"

"Yes."

"All right," conceded Jim. "I don't blame you. Who was he?"

"The man who shot Sheriff Nichol? He was a Mexican Hat cowboy. His name is Frank Holden."

"Brother," murmured Jim, "you better be able to prove that."

"Prove it?" said Sam Chavez, spreading his hands. "How can I prove it? I'll tell you what I know. The night of the shooting I went up to the saloon for a drink and afterward I went for a walk. It was a good night. Sometimes a man needs such a night for sorting out the things which become piled up in his mind over the weeks. I walked across the road and into the back alley, and stood for a while smoking back there, watching

102

how the stars seem sometimes to come closer, then run far out again. I also saw two cowboys riding down the west side of town but who pays attention to a pair of cowboys on such a beautiful night? Then I put out my smoke and started down the alleyway. My shop has a back door, you understand, and I live in the back room of my shop. I saw the two horses, only this time there was just one man with them. He was sitting his saddle, holding the reins to his friend's horse. I knew him, of course. He's been in my shop many times. Still, it came to me perhaps he didn't want to talk, so I started on. That's when the gunshot sounded. I ran over into the shadows. Who knows but what even a friend will kill a man for seeing too much?"

"Did you see the second one?" asked Lou.

"Yes. It was Frank Holden. And the one out there holding the horse, that one was Ewell Frith, superintendent of Mexican Hat."

"Frith?" said Jim, looking skeptical. "Chavez, why would a man like Frith go along on a lousy bushwhack? He could've sent any of his men."

"No," disagreed the old half-breed. "You don't know Mexican Hat, Sheriff. You think they are all bad men, but I know better. Mexican Hat hires only tough riders, but how many murderers can you find in a cow camp? Not very many. Killers, yes. There are killers all around you. But not murderers, and that's why Ewell Frith was along. He only wanted one other man to know, the man who pulled the trigger."

Bellanger looked thoughtfully at the saddle maker. Something was bothering Lou. "But why?" he asked

103

Chavez. "It was a Mexican Hat rider who tricked me . . . the same man Jim killed last night out in the road. I thought Mexican Hat and Bob Nichol were like two peas in a pod."

Chavez shrugged. "I don't know that. I'm only a saddle maker. I grew up not very far from Brigham. I've known Mexican Hat since it was first founded. I even rode for them many years ago as a young *vaquero*. It has always been a tough, rough outfit because it's had to be. There were things done back then, some of us didn't think were right, but since Bob Nichol has been sheriff there's been no trouble. I can't imagine why they shot him."

"Could you be mistaken?" asked Lou.

"No." The old man smiled. "I wasn't mistaken. I've already said it. Ewell Frith has been in my shop dozens of times. So has Frank Holden. And I was too close for the darkness to blur their faces. I saw them. I recognized them both. It was Frank who shot Bob Nichol, and Ewell Frith sat out there, holding Frank's horse, waiting for him to do it. That's what I saw. That's why I trailed after you tonight, in order to tell you, Sheriff Landon."

"Have you told anyone else?" asked Jim.

Chavez shook his head. "There was no one else to tell. There's been no peace officer since Bob was shot down." Chavez made that little self-effacing smile again. "Besides, how could I be sure who else might have been involved? All I had to do was open my lips to the wrong man . . . and *bang!*"

Jim stepped away from his horse, paced over to where Lou stood, turned, and gauged the saddle maker. After a while he said: "Sam, you seem to have a knack for seein' and hearin' things that could get you eliminated."

Chavez shook his head, more vigorously this time. "I saw nothing tonight. I heard nothing. Besides, you are the sheriff. Who would believe an old half-breed Mexican over the sheriff? Then, too, I know Lou Bellanger didn't shoot Sheriff Nichol, so what could I tell?"

Lou said: "Trust him, Jim. He's all right."

"How do you know that?" snapped London.

Lou said: "Because last night he had plenty of time to turn me in after he recognized me, and he didn't do it."

"Now you know why I didn't, too," said Chavez. "Because they'd have lynched you for shootin' Sheriff Nichol. I would've had an innocent man's blood on my hands."

Jim went back to his horse, tested the *cincha*, settled the reins, and swung up. From the saddle he said: "Sam Chavez, you better be damned careful how you get back to town. And after you get there, you'd better be even more careful. I'm not going to say a word of what you've told us here tonight, but Frith and those hardcase cowboys of his are no one to fool with."

London turned and departed from the barn out the back way, which was the same way he'd ridden in. For as long as Lou could hear the soft hoof falls of his withdrawing mount, he leaned in the darkness, saying

105

nothing. Out front, and southward, there was a light in the Hudsons' house. Elsewhere, the night was strongly quiet and warm.

Sam Chavez made a brown paper cigarette, popped it between his lips, but didn't light it. He had the match in his fingers ready to strike, but he stood perfectly still. You could see his light eyes, but that was about all. For a long while Sam stood, motionless, head slightly to one side, then he lowered the match, pocketed it, removed the unlit cigarette, and flung it aside as he said: "Listen, do you hear anything?"

Lou straightened up, ambled over into the doorway, and halted. He didn't hear a thing. Not even a distant coyote or a snorty horse restlessly slumbering out in the corral. He shook his head.

"Wait," murmured the old saddle maker, stepping out of the barn. "Wait. Pretty soon now you'll hear it."

"Hear what?"

"Horses. Be quiet and listen."

Lou remained quiet for some little time before he picked up something that wasn't actually a sound to be heard, so much as it was a sound to be felt in the air. A kind of pulsation, an oncoming reverberation that appeared to come more from the ground underfoot than from the overhead atmosphere. Old Sam showed his white teeth as Lou dropped his head a little.

"You pick it up now?" asked Chavez.

"Yeah. Horses. Sounds like they're a hell of a long way off, though."

"Yes. But they are coming this way, a lot of them. Maybe five or six men. You got an extra gun?"

Lou looked over. "Gun?"

Chavez answered a little exasperatedly: "Those men are riding straight for this place, Mister Bellanger. Those aren't loose horses. Men are riding them. What would men be night riding over here for, I wonder, except because of what everyone knows happened in this yard earlier?"

Lou turned with a ripped-out raw curse, jumped into his improvised room, and came back out with his carbine. As he handed it to Chavez, he said: "Where'd you leave your horse? You better get him an' fetch him inside the barn."

Chavez nodded and scuttled out into the darkness, ducking around the north side of the barn. Lou ran through and peered out back. He had no idea whether Jim London had already gotten too far away to hear this oncoming sound or not. He wished Jim hadn't left.

CHAPTER
NINE

They had plenty of time to get set. Even after those night riders got up close, they still didn't charge into the yard. Lou left old Sam Chavez in the barn and ran to the house to tell Jamie to turn out the lamps. He got back to Chavez and still those riders kept coming. It was easy to hear them now. In fact, the horsemen split up like a band of marauding Indians and charged down the west and east sides of the yard without firing a shot or raising a yell. Then they met southward on the range and did the same thing over again, charging up both sides of the yard. That time someone let off a shot at the house.

Lou heard glass break and splinter. He swore, ran over to the front barn opening, dropped to one knee, and tried mightily to sight someone out there in the darkness.

Sam Chavez finally heaved upright and leaned in the darkness out of harm's way and said: "I don't think they're goin' to come in. Listen, they are out there to the north getting ready for another charge. It's to terrify the people in the house."

Lou got back inside. Down through the total darkness of the barn's runway he could see the brighter range west of the ranch. "Come along," he growled. "Let's play a little game of our own."

Old Sam's white teeth showed. He was evidently enjoying all this.

Lou got out back. The horsemen to the north were beginning to split up again. They were beginning to ease their mounts over into a slow lope for the next charge down both sides of the yard. Lou looked left and right. On his left, which was southward, was the spidery substance of the Hudsons' network of pole corrals. This wasn't much cover; in broad daylight it would have been suicide to try anything from there. But the night would help, so Lou jerked his head and led Chavez over where they could both lie prone near a solid-planked runway used for spraying and doctoring cattle. Here, darkness lay like black molasses, inundating them both. The riders were returning. Lou pushed out his six-gun and cocked it. The range probably would be too great for a handgun, but Chavez had his carbine.

"Make it count," he said.

Chavez laid aside his old hat and chuckled. He dropped down, snugging back the Winchester for heft and feel, then he said, light eyes bright and youthful in his leathery old face: "A man thinks life had forgot him, left him behind a workbench in a gloomy shop. Then all of a sudden it turns out not to be so."

"You better hope they don't stop and fire back, because there's no place to roll from here," said Lou, and grinned back at Sam Chavez.

The riders came faster this time, as though wishing to reach the house quickly. Lou and Sam Chavez could see them, at last, as they swerved in closer. They had their six-guns up and ready. Apparently this time they meant to fire a full volley into the house. Lou picked out a man riding crouched, tracked him, and fired. Sam Chavez let loose with the carbine. Then old Sam did an odd thing; instead of raking backward and downward with his left hand to lever up the next cartridge, he held the carbine clear of his body and gave it a hard jerk downward, then upward. The levering mechanism worked automatically, slammed down and up again, and Sam was ready to fire once more without touching the cocking mechanism. It was a trick only an old hand with a Winchester saddle gun would know how to do properly. Sam slammed out his second shot, then his third and fourth ones, making the carbine in his hands thunder and buck in an almost continuous roar.

The shadowy horsemen out there were caught by surprise. They'd raced past the barn before, meeting only dark silence. This time it must have seemed as though a small army of gunmen were waiting. They cried out in sharp alarm and reined frantically away, but two horses ran loose, stirrups flapping and reins flying, their former riders lying back there, still and flat, in the gunpowder-scented night.

On the opposite side of the yard those other racing horsemen reached the house and poured a half-hearted volley into it as they sped past. For several minutes afterward there was the diminishing sound of riders passing southward. After that — silence.

Lou got up and reloaded. Sam Chavez eased down the hammer on Bellanger's carbine and turned to walk

110

back into the barn. He'd forgotten his hat that was lying in the dust. Lou called to him, picking up the hat. Sam came back. He seemed momentarily to have forgotten those two sprawled bodies out there.

"Cover me," said Lou. "Stand off to one side when you do it."

Chavez moved clear and carefully, walked over closer. One of the prone men moaned and Chavez cocked his Winchester. Lou looked quickly around at the mechanical sound before going on up and bending down to toss away the injured man's six-gun. He then stepped past and flopped the second man over. That one was dead, but not, apparently, from a gunshot wound. His neck was awkwardly bent. Evidently he'd been bucked off or had fallen from his horse when the firing started. However it had happened, the man was dead from a broken neck.

Lou went back to the injured cowboy, knelt, and eased him over. There was a long red splash low alongside the injured man's left side. Chavez came in, eased off the carbine, and bent down also to see.

"Broken ribs," he pronounced, and straightened up, gazing farther out. "How is the other one?"

"Dead," answered Lou. "His neck's busted. Give me a hand with this one into the barn."

The wounded cowboy was groggy. He tried to hold his head up, but failed. Neither could he manipulate his legs, so they had to half carry, half drag him over into the barn.

Lou sent Chavez to the house for cloth and a lantern. When the saddle maker returned, Judith

Hudson and Jamie came with him. Jamie was gripping his Winchester while Chavez had the lantern. Judith looked at the ragged wound and knelt beside the cowboy, white to the eyes, going right to work.

It took nearly an hour to get the injured man cared for. They were finishing up; the cowboy was coming around, grinding his teeth against the searing agony, when Sam Chavez went swiftly over to the doorway and listened, then turned and hissed for Lou to put out the light.

"Someone is coming from the direction of town," said Chavez, going once more after Lou's carbine. "It is only one man and he's coming fast."

Lou left Jamie and Judith with the wounded man. He blew out the light and went forward to take his position near the doorway. The rider slowed to a lope when he was several hundred yards out, and angled across the range straight toward the barn. When he was barely visible out there, he sang out.

"Hey down there . . . this is the sheriff. Don't shoot!"

Chavez looked at Bellanger.

Lou nodded. "That's his voice," he told the saddle maker, and stepped past to call back. "Ride on in, Jim, we're at the barn."

London's horse was dark with sweat when he slowed outside, stepped down, and flung one rein around the tie rack. "I heard shooting," he said, stepping swiftly forward. "It was back here at the ranch, but I was a damned long way toward town when I heard it. What happened?"

112

"Mexican Hat," said Lou bitterly. "There's a dead one out back and a hurt one in the barn. Come along."

Jim went inside where Chavez re-lighted their lamp. The Hudsons moved back and the injured man looked straight up. London glared at him.

"Who led you?" he asked. "Not Frith this time. Who was it?"

The cowboy closed his eyes, then sprang them wide open. He appeared to be having trouble making them focus. Lou bent over the man, straightened back, and shook his head. "He's half out of his head, Jim. He got a bad wound, a hard fall out there, and he's lost considerable blood."

Jim wasn't placated. "He's a Mexican Hat rider. I've seen him in town with other Mexican Hat men."

"That's no secret," muttered Bellanger.

London turned on him, his face wire-tight. "I told them to stay away from here. I told them that this afternoon when they brought Frith and their other hurt ones into town. Lou, I don't talk to hear the sound of my voice."

"Slow down," said Bellanger. "All right, you told them not to come around. But that doesn't mean they're goin' to obey you, Jim."

"Doesn't it? I've never been a sheriff before, Lou, but I know what a sheriff's supposed to do. First off, he's supposed to enforce the law. Well, I told 'em to stay away from the Hudson Ranch, and that's the law . . . my law!"

Judith Hudson came forward. "I can hitch the team," she said. "This man should be taken to Doctor Hart in town."

Jim turned, coldly angry, and started to say something, caught himself in time, and bit off the words. Sam Chavez had brought forth his horse and told them he should go back. No one stopped him, so Chavez departed. Jamie was trying to make a pillow for the wounded man with feed sacks. He was down on both knees muttering incoherently to himself as he did this. The lamp sputtered and smoked when a slight, vagrant, little, chilly breeze came blowing out of the northward night.

Jim London's fury subsided a little at a time. When Lou made a smoke and offered the makings, Jim accepted and, also, put his fingers to work. When Lou held the match, Jim lit up, then he said, blowing out smoke: "Mexican Hat!" He spat the words. "Maybe you were right an' I was wrong, Lou. Maybe I'll have to get emotionally involved in this, too. I told them to stay away from here."

"They stayed away, Jim. They tried to stay out just far enough so no one could identify them while they streaked down both sides of the yard. Their only mistake was in assuming I wasn't still around here, and that Sam Chavez wasn't here at all."

"Chavez," said London suddenly. "Did they recognize him?"

"Naw, they didn't recognize me, either. It was too dark. They were ridin' too hard, and we hit them like

114

half an army before they even knew there was anyone out in the night armed for them."

London looked past where Jamie and his wife were harnessing a team. "Go give 'em a hand," he said, and turned abruptly, walking back out of the barn. Lou started to obey, then turned back just in time to see London swing across leather, whirl his horse, and lope out of the yard in a north-westerly direction toward the headquarters ranch of Mexican Hat. He stood debating whether to go along, or whether to help the Hudsons and the injured man. In the end he went deeper into the barn to assist at getting the team onto the pole of the Hudsons' rickety, old, battered wagon.

They didn't speak to one another, even when they threw hay into the wagon box and lifted the wounded man to make him comfortable. But when he asked for water and Judith would have gone for it, Lou said: "No."

Judith turned back, looking up in a questioning manner. "He's hurt, Lou. He's suffering."

Lou nodded. "Good. Maybe the bouncing on the way to town will hurt some more. I've had a belly full of Mexican Hat. They ride roughshod over anyone they feel like pickin' on. Well, that's a boot that fits both feet. No water!"

Jamie looked bewildered. Lou said he could drive the rig, to get up on to the box and gather in the lines. Judith didn't argue with this order, but, as soon as Lou went striding back deeper into the barn after his saddle and his horse, she went after a pitcher of water for the injured cowboy. She was holding his head up while he

115

drank when Lou returned, mounted, and with his carbine in the saddle boot. She didn't look around when he reined to a halt beside the wagon box, but when she turned away, Lou was frostily regarding the cowboy.

"Mister, you're lucky she's a good woman. For my part all you're entitled to is a bullet."

The cowboy feebly raised a hand to wipe his lips. He said: "Bellanger, they're goin' to find you. They'll get you yet. No one believed you'd still be over here. But they'll get you, an' when they do . . ."

Lou signaled to Jamie to drive out, but Jamie turned on the box, looking uncertainly toward Judith. She hastened over, climbed up, and said something soothing to him. Then Jamie flicked the lines and the wagon lurched ahead.

Lou rode on the right side for a while, then scouted up ahead and waited. When the wagon appeared, he waved it on and fell in behind the tailgate. The Mexican Hat cowboy glared at him.

Lou said: "You make four of 'em accounted for so far. Another day or two and I'll double that. Only from now on . . . no more shoulder shots. From now on . . . killin' shots."

"They're goin' to get you, Bellanger," croaked the unrepentant range rider. "An' I got somethin' else to tell 'em, too. You 'n' that new lawman bein' friends. Wait'll folks hear about that!"

Lou rode along gazing at the injured man without saying a word until Brigham was in sight. It was late; the town lay on ahead of them darkly quiet and

116

shadowed. Lou hadn't wondered about the time until he saw that even the saloon was closed. He looked at the moon's position, guessed it had to be slightly past midnight, and speculated about what must be done to keep their injured prisoner from talking.

He rode up beside Jamie on the wagon's left side and said: "Head for the jailhouse, Jamie, not the doctor's house."

Judith leaned over. "Lou, he needs care right now."

"He'll get it, but at the jailhouse." He looked his mother in the eye. "That man back there knows Jim and I are friends. He knows we're all in this together. That's got to be kept from Mexican Hat as well as the local townsfolk. If they find out who Jim is, it'll upset everything. Jamie, you head for the jailhouse."

Jamie obeyed. He always obeyed anything that was said to him in a forceful manner. Judith leaned back, settling both hands in her lap. She made no further objections. They ground down into town setting up rough echoes as they rolled steadily and slowly through the empty roadway toward the jailhouse. When they stopped, Judith got down, walked back to look at the cowboy, then told Lou she was going after Dr. Hart, and hastened away.

CHAPTER
TEN

Conrad Hart was a long-legged, shag poke of a man whose age was around fifty or better, and whose medical background and training were exclusively homoeopathic. But he was an excellent diagnostician as well as general practitioner, and probably the one common ailment he was most adept at, after delivering babies, was caring for gunshot wounds.

As it turned out, long and lean and unhandsome old Dr. Hart was also an observant, shrewd, and knowledgeable man, for the moment he finished examining the wound in the Mexican Hat man's side, he squinted over at Bellanger and said: "Young man, if you'd been smart, you'd have kept right on going after the Sheriff Nichol affair. The longer a man tempts fate, the surer she is to chastise him. Now then, about this cowboy, we should take him down to my place where there's hot water and . . ."

"Doc," said Lou Bellanger, "this man stays right where he is until the sheriff gets back. You've looked at his wound. Will he make it all right without a lot of fancy bandagin'?"

Conrad Hart didn't hesitate. "Sure he'll make it. He's got two broken ribs and two fractured ones. No one dies from anything like that. But if I had him down at my place where I've got the carbolic acid and clean bandaging material, I could simply do a better job of caring for him."

The wounded man said: "Doc, I got to tell you something. I got to tell someone!"

Lou grabbed a chair, dragged it up close, and dropped down beside the bunk in the jailhouse cell where the wounded man had been laid out. He put his right hand lightly upon his right hip and sat impassively eyeing the prisoner. For a moment the cowboy seemed prepared to speak out despite that sulphurous look on Bellanger's face, but in the end he didn't utter another sound, he only sank back upon the pallet, shallowly breathing.

Dr. Hart gave Bellanger a wry look and stepped back. Lou raised his eyes finally. Hart said: "I see." He said that although not a word had passed between Lou and himself. "I see, young man, I'm a prisoner. Is that right?"

"If you weren't," said Lou, "how long would it take you to waken the town, Doc, and surround me in the jailhouse?"

Conrad Hart's brow wrinkled. "Oh, I'd say possibly fifteen minutes, young man. The folks hereabouts are hard sleepers. Take a while to get 'em up an' dressed an' armed ... providing I had any such asinine intention."

"Why asinine, Doc? You know who I am."

"I know who you are, of course. You're Bellanger. But I also happen to know that, if you were a murderer, you wouldn't have picked this jailhouse because eventually our new sheriff will be along."

The wounded cowboy rolled his eyes up at Dr. Hart and moved his lips, but Hart wasn't paying any attention to him. He was giving Lou Bellanger look for look.

"And, Bellanger, murderers don't bring wounded victims in at some personal peril, to save their lives."

Lou relaxed a little. "Anything else?" he asked, half mockingly.

"As a matter of fact there is," said Dr. Hart with the same force and spirit as he'd been speaking right along. "I happen to suspect you didn't shoot Sheriff Nichol."

Judith, in the shadowy background up until now, glided forward to hear better although both Bellanger and Hart were speaking in normal tones in a small, low-ceiling room.

"Go on," said Lou. "Let's have the rest of it, Doc."

"Ewell Frith was delirious after I bedded him down in my sanatorium, Mister Bellanger. He and Bob Nichol shared the same room. Bob is mending very well, and he called me in today to tell me Frith had said quite clearly while he was out of his mind that a Mexican Hat cowboy under Frith's orders and supervision had tried to kill Sheriff Nichol. Of course, Bob and I tried to get Frith to repeat this, but he never did. He lapsed into total unconsciousness. So you see, Mister Bellanger, there's an excellent reason for believing you didn't shoot Bob Nichol. Bob seems convinced you didn't, and that's good enough for me." Hart reared back. "Any other questions?"

120

Lou shook his head. "Just give me your word, Doc, you won't say a word to anyone until the sheriff gets back to town, then you'll let him handle this mess."

"You have my word, sir," snapped Hart, and groped around for his hat that he'd left in the outer office when he'd entered earlier. Jamie came in, vacantly smiling, holding the hat out. Conrad Hart took the hat and stood a moment, gazing at Jamie.

Lou turned. "Miz Hudson, keep watch on the prisoner. If he tries to get up or get out of here, tell Jamie to put him back down."

She nodded, looking worried. "Where are you going?"

"With the doctor up to talk to Sheriff Nichol . . . and Frith, if he'll talk."

"But . . . what about the sheriff?" she asked, clasping both hands over her stomach. "Will he come back?"

Lou crookedly smiled. "He'll come back. After all, ma'am, Mexican Hat's been losing men too fast lately to have more'n three or four left, if that many. And odds like those wouldn't even slow him down." He reached over, dropped a hand upon her shoulder, gave a gentle squeeze, then walked out into the front office where Hart was putting on his hat. "I'm goin' with you," he announced, and opened the door.

It was turning cold outside. The town was dark and ugly and endlessly slumbering all around them. Their footfalls set up small echoes as they paced northward. It was only an hour or two before sunup.

Dr. Hart, stork-like in appearance normally, was even more stork-like when he walked. He carried his head up and thrown slightly backward. His movements were jerky and deliberate. He gave the impression of being distant in thought whether he was or not, so when he spoke, finally, halfway up the deserted roadway, it caught all Lou Bellanger's attention at once.

"Bob Nichol and I have been friends a long time, Mister Bellanger. I know he's not the most popular peace officer in northern Arizona, but I also happen to know he's one of the best and most efficient peace officers, and I also happen to know he doesn't lie. He never lies."

Lou paced along, waiting. He, personally, would have made roughly the same syllepsis concerning Bob Nichol, but he didn't really know the man well enough to offer any kind of public utterance concerning him. Furthermore, this crane-like, self-trained medical man at his side was somewhat of an enigma in his own right, so Lou kept his eyes up and moving, alertly watching for movement anywhere around, and waiting for Conrad Hart to get it off his chest — whatever it was.

He didn't have much longer to wait. Dr. Hart said, when they were nearing the only house around with a light showing from parlor windows: "Bob Nichol told me he wasn't exactly surprised that Ewell Frith and Mexican Hat were involved in his attempted assassination."

This interested Lou. He'd faced every challenge that had come, knowing how to deal with all manner of violence, but he'd never stopped wondering about the oblique contingencies, particularly this one, so he said: "What did he tell you?"

122

Conrad Hart stepped in front of Bellanger, threw open a little picket gate with a flourish, and waved Lou on in. "He'll be awake, Mister Bellanger. I'll let him explain it for himself."

Inside, the stove had recently been stoked and the house was warm. Almost too warm, in fact, and it was also stuffy until Hart led Lou into a large airy bedroom where two lamps burned steadily, and Bellanger saw Bob Nichol propped up in one bed, and ten feet closer to the south wall, Ewell Frith lying in gray and motionless quiet.

Dr. Hart jerked his head and said in his dry way: "Brought you a visitor, Sheriff. Lou Bellanger, the man folks want to hang for bushwhacking you."

Lou and hard-eyed Bob Nichol exchanged a glance that was neither warm nor amiable. Hart stepped past to the second bed and looked down. Sheriff Nichol rolled his head over and said: "More of the same, Con. He's out of his head. You know, I'm disappointed. I'd always figured Ewell Frith to be a tough customer."

"He's tough, all right," put in Lou Bellanger, swinging up a chair to sit upon. "I'm the one who shot him out front of the Hudsons' house. He was pretty close and the slug knocked him out of the saddle. If he wasn't tough, he'd also be dead, Sheriff." Lou waited a moment to let this phase of the talk die, then he said: "Did you know Frank Holden shot you and that man over there in the other bed held the horses and waited for Holden to do it?"

"No," stated Bob Nichol candidly. "I knew Frith was involved because he muttered about it in his delirium, but I didn't know it was Frank who did the shooting. How do you know that?"

"A man here in town saw it happen. He told a couple of us tonight."

Nichol's hard gaze lingered on Bellanger's tired features. "Us?" he murmured. "Who is us? You and that other professional gunfighter?"

Lou's stare flattened out. "Who you talkin' about, Sheriff?"

"Hell," growled Nichol. "You know perfectly well whom I'm talking about. Sheriff Jim Landon. *Humph!* I saw him out the window last evenin'. His name's London not Landon. I've seen that face a hundred times on flyers. Two-Gun Jim London. Only around here he's only wearin' one gun."

Bellanger let his breath out in a quiet sigh and shifted his attention. "You knew?" he asked Dr. Hart. The medical man nodded and bent down to do something to Ewell Frith's bandages.

Lou gazed in mild puzzlement at Sheriff Nichol. "If you knew yesterday, Sheriff, how come you didn't secretly organize the town against him?"

"That's no mystery," gruffly stated Bob Nichol. "I also heard what he told the men from Mexican Hat who brought Frith in and left him, and who took their other wounded back to the ranch with them. He said the next time Mexican Hat hit the Hudson Ranch, he was goin' to lift someone's scalp. And that, Bellanger, is just exactly what I was on the edge of doing when they shot me down. Let London go on. So far he's done just right."

124

"He's an outlaw, Sheriff."

"*Humph!* So are you an outlaw, Bellanger. But not around here, and it just happens that it's what happens around here that matters most to me. Why did they shoot me? I'll tell you. Because they had to. They meant to hit the Hudsons, shoot them down or drive them off or burn them out, and they couldn't do it as long as I could ride. They knew that. So they plugged me, then hit the Hudson place, but in the meantime something else had happened. You and Two-Gun Jim London had shown up. It's a mystery to me how you two happened along precisely at the right time, but I believe in a good fate as well as a bad one, Bellanger, so I'll just leave it like that."

When Sheriff Nichol finished speaking, Lou looked up and saw Dr. Hart watching him. Lou said: "Well, I didn't have to insist that wounded one down there at the jailhouse be kept from shooting off his mouth, after all. You already knew. In fact, you knew more than I thought you did. Both of you. And it's true, I'm in this with Jim London."

"That wounded cowboy knows, is that it?" asked the doctor.

"Yeah, they hit the Hudson place again tonight. That one got winged. There's still one more of them out there. Only he's dead. You can send for him any time you're of a mind, Doc." Lou stood up, dropped a thoughtful gaze upon Bob Nichol, and said: "Sheriff, after they hit the Hudson place tonight, when Jim London had told them to stay away from there, Jim was pretty mad. He rode out to Mexican Hat. That's been a couple hours back. What are his chances, out there? You reckon it'd help if I went out to sort of lend a hand?"

Nichol rolled his head negatively on the pillow. "Not after two hours," he muttered. "In that length of time they're either burying him, or he's on his way back to town."

Lou nodded. "One more question, Sheriff. Now that we've knocked Ewell Frith out of it, who's ramroddin' things?"

"Lacey Shafter. He's part owner of Mexican Hat. He and his sister, Stacey Shafter, own the whole shootin' match. Lacey's been livin' at the ranch this past year. His sister lives back East."

"So it'll be this Lacey Shafter who'll be pushing the fight for Miz Hudson's water rights."

Nichol nodded, rolled his head over, and said: "Doc, how's Jamie?"

Hart's mouth dropped. "Saw him at the jailhouse a while back, Bob. He's the same. He hasn't had a rational moment in six months, as far as I know, and you know what I told you. With brain damage like he had, the only sign of mend would be whether he had recurrin' rational moments which came closer an' closer together. While if he went the other way, it'd mean he'd be regressin' further and further from any recovery of his wits at all."

"Whoa," said Lou. "Jamie had a long talk with me yesterday. He was as sane as you or me, Doc." Nichol and Conrad Hart looked intently at Bellanger. Neither of them said anything, so Lou recalled that long conversation he'd had with Jamie out front of the barn, just before Mexican Hat hit the ranch. Hart got a relieved expression across his features. So did Bob Nichol. The doctor tugged out a big gold watch, glanced at it, gave his head a tired little shake, then said he'd walk back down to the jailhouse with Lou. He wanted to talk to Judith and Jamie Hudson.

Outside, the eastern sky was turning a green shade, like the murky depths of the ocean. False dawn was upon the land. The cold was more pronounced now, but this was the shank of the night. As soon as the sun came, so, also, would the warmth come.

Down at the livery barn a hostler was bustling around, refilling troughs and buckets and whistling as he worked. But that was the only sign of life in town, just yet. Dr. Hart watched the youthful hostler and yawned. He evidently hadn't been to bed at all. "Sure would be fine," he muttered, "if folks always felt as good at dawn as that lad down there, wouldn't it, Mister Bellanger?"

Lou nodded. Except for the uncertainty about what had happened out at Mexican Hat, he didn't feel too badly, a little wrung out because it had been a long and strenuous night, but otherwise not bad at all.

"You think Jamie'll pull out of it, maybe?" he asked.

Hart made a little grimace. "I've doctored him an' I've prayed. Now all I can do is wait, Mister Bellanger . . . and hope."

CHAPTER
ELEVEN

Jim London arrived back in Brigham just as the sun was making its majestic rise beyond the farthest horizon. He left his horse at the livery barn and entered the jailhouse without a word. He saw the people in there and nodded, then, still without speaking, jerked his head for Lou Bellanger to accompany him back outside.

There was a trickle of roadway traffic, finally, but so far the day's business hadn't gotten quite under way yet. Across the road and northward several doors, Merritt Burgess's clerk was sweeping the boardwalk. Up by the Trail Saloon two derelicts stolidly waited.

London saw all this and thumbed back his hat as he ran a wry, cursory glance all around, then said: "Well, I had my say out there, and Lacey Shafter . . . the owner . . . had his say." Jim looked around. "Mexican Hat, Lou, is a Mexican stand-off."

"Shafter wouldn't quit?"

London gave a hard, little, explosive laugh. "Quit? He told me he's already sent south for some gun hands. He said he'd been fair an' reasonable an' even accommodating to the Hudsons, and now he was goin' to take off the gloves."

128

Bellanger's brow wrinkled. "Fair? Accommodating?"

London nodded. "That's what he called it. So I told him, if that's the way he wanted it, that's how he was goin' to get it." London paused, then said: "You know what he did, Lou? He dared me to arrest him." Jim chuckled. "I've never arrested anyone in my life. I've been too busy keepin' out of the way of other men trying to do that to me to even learn what words a feller uses. So I told him the facts of life. I wouldn't arrest any more Mexican Hat riders. I'd shoot them."

"He let you ride away after you said that?"

"Well, not exactly. You see, I'd walked him out to where my horse was, and his men were in the cook shack being fed breakfast."

Bellanger hung his head. "I wish it'd stayed simple like before," he muttered. Then he remembered something and raised his face. "Sheriff Nichol knows I didn't shoot him. He's up at the pill-pusher's place, abed. Frith's up there with him. They also know who you are."

"That so?" muttered Jim London, completely unconcerned. "Lou, I never got it out of Shafter how these gunmen are going to arrive in town or when, exactly, he expects them. So I figure we'd better organize ourselves a little reception committee. You go around back where folks won't get too good a look at you, and talk Chavez into keeping watch from his harness shop front window. I'll go see about gettin' Burgess and maybe that disagreeable cuss up at the Trail to do the same. Those men'll either arrive on the stage, or they'll come on horseback. The trick's goin' to be to be right on top of them the moment they step down into the dust. I'll also pass the word down at the livery barn." London thought a moment, found all this satisfactory, and returned his attention to the present. "How's that shot-up cowboy?"

"In a cell," replied Lou. "He's goin' to be all right. But we can't let him get out where he'll tell the whole damned town you and I are friends."

London agreed. He also cautioned Lou about being seen, now that people were beginning to appear in greater numbers up and down the roadway. Then he turned and stepped out into the roadway, sauntering on over in the direction of Burgess's general store.

Lou went around to the back alley behind the jailhouse, down it to the back entrance to Chavez's saddle shop, and let himself in without a sound. The saddle maker was nursing a mug of black coffee and softly smiling to himself as though in recollection of something pleasing or amusing, or both. When Lou spoke, Chavez turned, unruffled, and said: "I thought maybe one of you would come see me. I saw the sheriff walk by a little while ago."

"Mexican Hat has hired some gunfighters," explained Lou. "We want you to keep watch out your front window. They'll arrive on horseback or on the stage, but we don't know when, so if you see any strangers . . ."

"I understand," said the saddle maker, and lifted an edge of his canvas apron to disclose a holstered six-gun tied to his right leg. He looked a little diffident about

130

this, and self-consciously smiled. "Well, an old man feels not so old. You understand?"

Lou nodded. "Sure. But be careful, Sam. Don't do anything. I'll be at the jailhouse. We brought in that wounded one from the Hudson place. He's in a cell up there. If you see anyone who might fit the description, walk on up and let us know."

Chavez pointed to his coffee pot on the little sheet-iron stove at the back of the shop, but Lou shook his head and went out into the back alley again, walked around to the front of the jailhouse, and very nearly met disaster there. As he stepped out on to the plank walk, Elmer Beadle from the Trail Saloon came swinging along, southward bound. Lou dropped his head, loosened his shoulders, and went shuffling past as though he were an older, dark-skinned man, and it worked. Elmer threw him an indifferent glance, hiked right on past, and didn't turn to gaze back as Lou stepped into the jailhouse. It was too close, Lou told himself. Now that full daytime was over the land, he'd have to hole up.

Judith and Jamie were inside, waiting. Jamie was handling one of the sawed-off shotguns from the office wall rack. When Lou saw that, Judith told him the weapon wasn't loaded. He moved farther into the room, her eyes following him. He went over to peer through the yonder door where the wounded cowboy lay upon his pallet in the cell. The range man said: "They'll still get you, Bellanger. They'll have the whole blessed countryside after you directly, you wait an' see."

131

Lou nodded, turned, and went back over where Judith was sitting, small and sturdy and forlorn. He dropped down beside her on the bench, pushed out his long legs, and leaned back. He was tired.

"What will you do when all this is over?" she softly asked, watching his face.

He looked at her, looked over at Jamie, then dug around for his makings. "It's not over. I never plan too far ahead. It's best, I've found, to live this life a day at a time." He worked up the smoke, popped it between his lips, and struck the match.

"Louis, I want to go see the children. They're staying with friends only a little ways from here. Would it be all right, do you suppose?"

"Sure," he said, exhaling a gray streamer. "Take Jamie."

At the sound of his name being spoken, Jamie set the shotgun back in its slot and turned. "I'd better stay here," he said, looking straight at Lou Bellanger. "You don't know Mexican Hat. You may think hurting them twice and shooting Ewell Frith will slow them down, but Judith and I know better."

Lou gazed across the room through slitted eyes, with smoke rolling upward in front of his face. Beside him, Judith stiffened a little; he could feel her do it on the bench. She, too, was watching Jamie. He walked over and smiled down at her.

"You go stay with the young ones," he said in a soft and pleasant tone. "I'll stay here because just these two can't stop Mexican Hat, Judith."

Obviously Jamie was having one of his lucid moments. Judith groped for a little, balled-up handkerchief. Lou stood up, suddenly, and went across to a window, looked out, turned with his back to the wall, and studied the pair of older people. He dropped his cigarette, stamped on it, and took one more look out the window before saying he thought Judith should leave the jailhouse. Jamie agreed with him and helped her arise. He held her by the elbow across to the door, which Bellanger reached down to open. As she passed him, Lou said: "Don't fret. We'll be just fine in here. Jim'll be back directly, too."

"They'll do *something*," she said earnestly. "Even without Ewell Frith, they'll find out where you are and do something, Louis."

Lou studied the tired, wan face and kept silent. If he had been someone else rather than her son, it would have been much easier for them both, for all of them, Jim and Jamie included. But that possibility, if it ever existed, was something that belonged to another plausibility. It had nothing to do with here and now. He said: "Go see the kids, ma'am. We'll be all right. These are right stout walls." Jamie took her outside and returned. Bellanger closed the door, watching Jamie. He began to understand something he hadn't had much time to speculate about before. When Jamie was lucid, his expression was different, his mouth was straighter and thinner, neither loose nor soft-seeming. His eyes focused with a brighter intensity; the opaqueness wasn't there. That's how he'd looked the day before in front of the Hudsons' barn. That was how he looked now.

Lou recalled what Dr. Hart had said. If the lucid moments came closer together, it meant the healing process inside Jamie's head was proceeding normally. Well, there'd been a lucid moment the day before, and there was another lucid moment now.

Lou said: "Jamie, how good's your memory?"

He got a perfectly rational answer. "About as good as most memories, I reckon. Why?"

"The day they beat you up . . . can you recall any of it?"

"Some. I was whistling, so I didn't hear them, but when my team looked around, so did I. Frith and Holden and Bell Forrester. I saw them all dismounting. Frith told me I was making fence on Mexican Hat land. I told him that wasn't so. Bell swore at me . . ."

Lou waited, but Jamie went silent. Evidently that was all he recalled. But it was enough. Maybe it wouldn't have held up in a law court, but the way Lou Bellanger and Jim London, and hundreds of professional dispute-settlers like them throughout the West were concerned, it would never get to a law court anyway.

Two men came striding down the plank walk and turned in at the jailhouse. Jim London and Conrad Hart. Jamie opened the door for them and smiled at Dr. Hart. Jim London brushed on past, but not Hart. He stood a moment, gazing into Jamie's eyes, then took him by the arm and led him over to a far window. Jim turned his back on them both and told Lou he'd set up a fair crew of watchers up and down the main roadway.

He then looked around and asked where Judith Hudson was. Lou told him. Jim thought on that a moment and shrugged, as though to imply it was perhaps for the best. He asked if Lou were hungry.

"Just tired," answered Bellanger.

They discussed which course to follow: await whatever Mexican Hat might try next, or get up a posse and go out and arrest Lacey Shafter. Jim laughed at that. "You know," he said, "I maybe could develop a taste for being a lawman, Lou. Look at all the help you get, an' how folks look up to you."

"That's middle age speaking," said Dr. Hart, strolling toward the cell room and leaving Jamie over by the front window. "It hits us all sooner or later, Sheriff. When a man starts thinking of his future, and of social acceptance . . . all those things which go with both . . . he's getting along toward middle age."

London eyed Hart without comment. After the medical man had passed on into the cell room, he began making a smoke thoughtfully. He was still like that when Sam Chavez stepped in off the front sidewalk, beckoned, and crossed beside the small front window where Jamie was still standing. Lou followed Jim across the room. Sam hadn't said a word. He didn't say one now, as he lifted an arm and pointed out three dusty horsemen riding abreast up the center of the roadway from the south end of town. He didn't have to say anything.

Jim London looked out, studied the three strangers, then completed his cigarette, struck a match on the seat of his trousers, and turned toward the wall rack. "Help yourself," he told Chavez and Jamie. "Lou, suppose we just step outside and meet these fellers."

Bellanger had taken the measure of the slow-walking mounted men out there, too. He knew what they were even though he'd never before laid eyes on any of them. He reached down, flicked off the tie down to his belt gun, told Conrad Hart who was just coming back into the office to remain inside, and trooped out of the jailhouse two steps behind Jim London.

The roadway was bright and hot and redolent of roiled dust. The traffic was mostly farther northward, up in front of Burgess's store, and even farther up than that, where other business houses were doing business. Out front of the jailhouse there was no roadway traffic, although across the way several men were standing in the overhang shade out front of a beanery, sucking their teeth and talking. They had evidently just had their morning meal.

The three-abreast riders were taking in the sights as they walked their horses northward. They were obviously strangers to Brigham. Lou made a narrow study of the men before he and Jim stepped off the plank walk. "Border men," he said. "Mex horns on two of those saddles and plenty of silver on the spurs and bits. Maybe Texans."

Jim nodded, having apparently arrived at just about this same judgment. He, also, loosened the gun on his hip in its holster, watching the riders pass the livery barn, the barbershop, and bakery. "They get a choice," Jim said. "Jail or shoot-out. If we just run them off, they'll cut around town and head for Mexican Hat."

Up by the Trail Saloon someone whistled, high and loud. It was clearly a warning, at least Jim and Lou took it to be one, and turned quickly. Coming into town from the north end were more riders. Lou recognized only one of them.

"Frank Holden," he said. "Hell, I thought that hole in his shoulder would put him down for a while."

"See that curly-headed big feller out front?" said Jim. "That's Lacey Shafter." London made a little snorting sound. "So the strangers didn't just arrive in Brigham," he mused. "Well, this sort of changes things. Lou, step between the buildings up yonder. I'll brace Shafter's hired guns and you take care of Shafter himself. It's that or tuck tail, and I've spouted off too much to Shafter to run now. Go on, walk over there before any of them get close enough to cut you off."

Lou moved lightly, walking with swift, sure strides as far as the place Jim had indicated. There, he faded from sight between two buildings, drew his handgun, spun the cylinder once, then breathed deeply and waited.

CHAPTER
TWELVE

Two shotguns, their black, twin barrels in steady hands, appeared out the jailhouse front windows, one on each side of the doorway. That was what stopped those three gunfighters before Jim London first stepped down into the golden-lighted roadway. There was no mistaking the intent of those scatter-guns and the distance was just about right. The mounted men reined up, lowered their rein hands, and sat like stone, eyeing those big-bored weapons. Farther back up the road, in front of the Trail Saloon, the Mexican Hat horsemen also slowed and stopped, but they couldn't see the shotguns. All they saw was Jim London stepping away from the sidewalk down in front of the jailhouse. It was the curly-headed, stocky man out front, the one London had identified to Lou Bellanger as being Lacey Shafter, who stopped the men up the roadway. Shafter undoubtedly meant to stay back so that his hired guns would have clear shooting with small danger of inadvertently winging the wrong man.

London's frock coat was tucked nearly under his gun belt, his hat was tipped down to shade his eyes, and, when he halted, turning to face the three horsemen, there was no mistaking his purpose or his intention. He was a gunfighter ready to prove his worth.

The three strangers were rough, unshaven, sweat- and travel-stained men, lean and darkly tanned and empty faced. The one in the middle said: "Well, Sheriff, looks like a right thoughtful reception you got lined up for us."

London's answer was in the same flat, quiet drawl. "Depends on you, boys. Lead pellets at a hundred and fifty feet, or a jail cell."

The youngest of those three men leaned upon his saddle horn. He was bold and blue-eyed, and juiceless, but he had youth, which meant he had perfect co-ordination and speed. He said, speaking down to Jim London: "Sheriff, unless you got a hold notice on us from somewhere else, I don't see how you aim to jail us. Hell, we just rode into your bailiwick."

"Sure you did," stated Jim. "And those other riders back up the roadway behind me . . . they just happened to ride into town at the same time, didn't they? Youngster, you better come up with something better than that."

"You figure I ought to, do you?" exclaimed the youth, drawing back his lips in a cold grin. "Well now, Sheriff, you ain't in too good a spot yourself, us in front, them other boys behind. In fact, if I was in your boots, about now I'd be tryin' to remember some prayers my mammy taught me."

Jim gazed scornfully at this one, saying: "Sonny, those shotguns over there will splatter your lousy innards all the way across the road on the store fronts,

139

if they go off. You think it over a minute, then tell me who you figure's in the worst position."

The older, heavier man in the center said from the corner of his mouth: "Ease off, Boyd." Then he raised his voice slightly. "Sheriff, all we want is a little cold beer an' a bait of grain for the horses. That's all. We're just passin' through."

"Yeah, I know," said London. "Passin' through as far as those men up in front of the saloon behind me, Mexican Hat. Mister, you got a choice. Draw, or dismount and walk over inside that damned jailhouse."

There was one of the gunfighters who hadn't said a word so far. He was one of those leathery, wispy individuals whose age could have been twenty-five or forty-five. The only factor that would have made it unlikely he was the latter age was that men in his line of work didn't live to reach forty-five. He spoke up now, for the first time, looking with a little troubled frown down at Jim London.

"Sheriff, I got a feelin' we've met before. I keep thinkin' there's somethin' about you . . ."

Jim brushed that aside. "You'll have plenty of time to think on it in a cell," he stated.

Up the road that unseen man whistled again, loud and long. London stiffened but he didn't so much as turn his head. He couldn't; he had three hired killers in front of him. But he undoubtedly heard those Mexican Hat horsemen up there starting to walk their horses on down southward behind him. Whatever thoughts passed through London's mind didn't show on his face at all. He watched the travel-stained hired gunmen, and

140

they in turn eyed him with the gentle certainty of men who thought they had just encountered something that was going to ensure their safety — when they killed.

That was before Lou Bellanger stepped from between two buildings, walked almost casually out into the roadway, and turned, facing the men from Mexican Hat. Lou's back was no more than 100 feet from the back of Jim London.

"That'll be far enough," Bellanger said.

The curly-headed, blocky rider who was slightly in the lead held up his hand. He stopped. So did the men on each side and back a short distance behind him. Frank Holden, with his left arm in a sling and his left shoulder bulky beneath the shirt with bandaging, said: "Hell, that's Bellanger." He didn't say it loud, but it carried up and down the suddenly empty roadway and into the doorways and open windows where people breathlessly watched.

For ten seconds no one made a move or a sound. Eventually the curly-haired man said: "Bellanger, eh? Some men live and learn, Bellanger, and some just live. Looks to me like you've forfeited even that right."

"Well, now," Lou said softly, glaring straight at Lacey Shafter, "if you want to prove that statement, Curly, just move your right hand off the saddle horn."

Shafter didn't move his right hand. Neither did any of the men around him. Over in front of Merritt Burgess's store the paunchy, big proprietor shouldered through the men pressing back into his recessed doorway. Burgess had a long-barreled fowling rifle in his hands. His face was pale and sweat-dappled, but it was grim and resolute as well.

In front of the saddle shop, which was a little distance to the rear of the three men facing Jim London, old Sam Chavez stepped out with his cocked six-gun. Across the way an old, white-haired character with a buffalo carbine stepped forward, hooked his thumb around an overhang post, and laid the carbine across his braced forearm. The bore of that buffalo gun was larger than the end of a man's thumb. At close range, the way it was pointed, it would tear a mounted man in half.

Farther back, up in front of the Trail Saloon, Elmer Beadle walked out with a six-gun in each hand. Two cowboys standing up there, watching, went down to their horses at the tie rack, dragged out carbines, and wordlessly followed Elmer out into the roadway. There, the pair of range riders both knelt, raised their weapons and cocked them, and what had, moments before, seemed to be a hopelessly one-sided impending fight suddenly became something altogether different.

Jim London didn't raise his voice as he said, staring up at the three motionless gunfighters: "Get down!" The strangers sat a long moment, watching Jim. Finally the man in the middle inclined his head, loosened his right foot, and swung down on the left side of his mount. The other two gunmen also got down and stood, the younger one obeying the slowest and, after he was down, hooking his left hand in the front of his belt.

"Shed those guns!"

This time the gunmen hung fire. Being disarmed by one man in front of an entire town was the worst thing that could happen to men whose reputations were all that kept them alive and in business.

"Boys," Jim London said conversationally, "I know how you feel. It doesn't make a damned bit of difference here and now, though. Drop the guns or get dropped."

Again the husky gunman, the one with his friends on either side of him, made the first move. And, also again, the youngest gunfighter obeyed last. His eyes were glazed with killing fury and impotence. He looked up where Jamie and Dr. Hart had him under their jailhouse scatter-guns. He even twisted a little and saw Sam Chavez standing back there aiming straight at him. He ripped out a curse and dropped his weapon.

Jim London didn't move for a while. He deeply breathed, loosened in the legs and shoulders a little, and said over his shoulder without looking around: "Lou, how you makin' it?"

Bellanger's answer was soft. "Fine, Jim. Just fine. I'm goin' to give Mexican Hat their one chance, too." Lou waited. He let the silence run on until it was stretched tight. He stared straight at Lacey Shafter, holding the older man's glance until, eyeball to eyeball, Shafter blinked. Then Lou said: "Curly, turn that horse. Take those cowboys with you an' ride right on back out of town just like you rode in. And, Curly . . . one more thing. Next time come shootin', or without any gun around your middle. You understand?"

Shafter turned his horse. He was brick-red. If it had been hard for the strangers to be disarmed and glared down out in the center of the roadway of Brigham with half the population looking on, it was doubly hard for the owner of the biggest and toughest cow ranch in the Brigham countryside.

Up the road Elmer Beadle growled at his bleak companions and walked back to the edge of the roadway, leading them. As the Mexican Hat riders walked their horses past, Elmer said: "Don't a blessed one of you ever so much as step your feet inside my saloon again. An' that goes double for you, Frank Holden!"

Sam Chavez holstered his gun and sauntered over to take charge of the gunmen's horses. "I'll lead them down to the livery barn," he told Jim, and turned, tugging the horses after him.

Across the road that old, white-maned character with the buffalo gun straightened up, lowered his weapon, and said: "Sheriff Landon, I'm the feller who's keepin' Judith's an' Jamie's chil'en for 'em. Me 'n' the missus. Just thought I'd mention it so's you'd know you wasn't entirely alone." The old man didn't wait for an answer; he turned and went trudging away.

That unarmed gunman, who'd seemed trying to recall something about Jim, gave his head a quick little bird-like jerk up and down. "Landon," he said. "Hell, yes. On'y it ain't Landon, it's . . ."

"Big-mouth," said Dr. Hart from his jailhouse window. "Did you ever hear of a man's finger bein' so sweaty it slipped off the trigger accidentally-like?"

The gunman didn't seem to understand exactly what that meant, but he had no difficulty at all in understanding when Conrad Hart lowered his shotgun barrels and held them straight on the man's middle. Not another word was said by this gunfighter.

Lou turned and walked over beside Jim London. He looked smokily at their prisoners. "Well, you called it, Jim. Dead or locked up."

London was wry. "For a spell there I wasn't so darned sure which." He gestured at the unarmed gunfighters. "Inside the jailhouse, boys. Walk in easy-like and, if you've got hide-out guns, don't be foolish because I'll be right behind you."

The ringleader of those strangers trooped over and obediently entered the jailhouse. Ten feet past the door he stopped, facing Jamie and Dr. Hart, each with cocked riot guns. He turned on Jim and said: "What in the hell are all those folks afraid of, Sheriff? I swear, in all my borned days I never had so many blessed guns pointed at me with white faces behind 'em."

Lou stepped out, gave the ringleader a rough push toward the back wall, and ordered the other two: "Line up. Put your hands over your heads on the wall and push. *Push*, damn you!" Lou went over them minutely and came away with two boot knives and one under-and-over Derringer.

Jim London tossed down his stiff-brimmed hat, arranged his coat so it was no longer tucked behind his hip holster, and started to make a smoke. He had nothing to say to the captives until he had the cigarette lighted. "Spill it out," he then said. "How much did

Lacey Shafter agree to pay you, and who'd he want killed?"

"Sheriff," said the ringleader of the gunmen, "you got us all wrong. We . . ."

"Never mind," grumbled the shorter, slighter-built man who'd tried to speak before, out in the roadway. "Jess, that feller's no more a sheriff than I am. Hell's bells, don't you recognize him? That there's Two-Gun Jim London!"

Even the arrogant, youthful gunfighter got big-eyed now. The three of them stood staring, and Jim went right on smoking his cigarette. "Lou," he said. "Would you mind lockin' 'em up?"

Bellanger smiled, crossed to the cell-room door, and growled. The prisoners turned, still glancing around at Jim, hatless, frock-coated, smoking his cigarette in front of the old roll-top desk, then, when Lou growled a second time, they trooped on into the cell room, obediently and thoughtfully. Just as Lou finished locking them into a cell adjoining the cell where the injured cowboy lay sound asleep on his pallet, the youngest gunman sidled up and said: "Tell me, mister, is that *really* Two-Gun Jim London?"

Lou didn't answer. He didn't even look up until he'd finished locking the cell door, then he paused only long enough to cast a withering glance at the three prisoners, and walked back out into the office, slammed the door at his back, and flung the keys upon the desk. After all that, he finally removed his hat, blew out a big breath, and looked over where London was grinning at him. Whatever he might have said was broken off

146

unuttered as Elmer Beadle barged in from outside, still with two six-guns stuffed in the front of his barman's apron, carrying a bottle of rye whiskey and two glasses.

At sight of Dr. Hart and Jamie, Elmer looked momentarily flustered, then, settling the liquor atop the desk, he said: "Well, you boys can sort of spell off usin' the glasses. I didn't know there was anyone else inside here."

Beadle beamed on them all, turned, and marched back outside again, where the first soft shadows of afternoon were beginning to creep out up and down the roadway. Men and women stood everywhere, in front of stores, on the edge of the sidewalks, even out in the dusty roadway, feverishly talking and gesturing. Lou Bellanger and Two-Gun Jim London — with only one gun this time — had backed down nearly eight armed men, all tooled up and itching for a showdown. History had been made in the town of Brigham this day.

Inside the jailhouse the men who'd made that history soberly drank, passed on the glasses, and scarcely looked straight at one another at all.

CHAPTER
THIRTEEN

"Maybe," said Dr. Hart, refusing the second drink of whiskey, "we should've locked up Frank Holden, too, Sheriff."

Jim shook his head. "Doc, we took three an' that was a damned sight more close than you know. If we'd tried for one more, the fireworks would have erupted."

Hart said: "All right, I reckon you know best in these matters. But Frank Holden's proved himself to be, in my opinion, the lowest-down kind of whelp in the world . . . a bushwhacker!"

Lou finished off his second drink and handed the bottle to Jamie. "Don't you worry about Frank Holden," he told Conrad Hart. "Every man like Holden gets to the end of his rope someday. I've got a feeling Frank's about at the end of his rope, too."

That could have been a threat. Coming from a professional gunfighter such as Lou Bellanger was, it could also be an epitaph. Dr. Hart seemed inclined to accept it as the latter, and therefore put Holden out of his mind and said he thought Sheriff Landon ought to make up a posse and go settle with Mexican Hat. Before London could answer, if in fact he'd meant to, Merritt Burgess and several other townsmen barged

148

into the little office, making it just about as full of large men as it could be.

Burgess told Jim and Lou the town of Brigham owed them both a debt of gratitude. He looked straight at Lou and said: "We just had a long talk with Bob Nichol. He saw what happened through a window up at Doc's house. Mister Bellanger, we owe you a full apology. We sure thought you'd shot Bob, like Bell Forrester said, out of spite."

"Forrester had a reason for wanting the blame to be put on Bellanger," stated Jim London. "It almost worked, too."

Conrad Hart had his long, skinny arm across the shoulders of Jamie Hudson. He said he thought he'd take Jamie over where Judith and their children were, then maybe drift on up home to tend to his sick patients. The others moved aside for the doctor and Jamie to pass through. Lou made a point of smiling at Jamie so Hudson would look straight up at him. Jamie obliged. His eyes still had that bright, interested look in their depths. Lou raised a thick arm, gave Jamie a soft pat across the back, and fell to making a smoke.

After those two had departed, Merritt Burgess told Jim London he and the other townsmen had discussed the recent showdown up at Elmer's bar, and had unanimously come to the conclusion that, whatever action Sheriff Landon wanted to take against Mexican Hat, the townsmen would stand foursquare behind him.

Jim thanked them all, held the door for them to walk out, and smiled at each townsman as he went past. Lou was dryly smiling when Jim finally closed the door and set his back against it, looking tired. Lou said: "You just might really be gettin' a taste for this life, after all. The way you smiled and bowed to every one of those storekeepers as you let 'em out the door made me wonder if maybe you weren't figurin' on runnin' for governor of the territory."

"Oh, go to hell," muttered London, went to the desk, sat down, and rummaged in his coat pockets for a cigar. He found it, lit up, and leaned far back watching Lou. "Don't make fun of 'em, Lou, because we're going to need them. First thing in the morning we're going to get us up a posse and go clean out Mexican Hat."

Bellanger eased down upon the wall bench. "Suits me," he said. "If I'd had my way, we'd have cleaned 'em out when we had 'em in the roadway a while back."

"Naw, they'd have had those two-bit gunfighters to help 'em. Maybe they wouldn't have gotten you 'n' me in the fracas, but they'd sure as hell would have killed a passel of the local folks. Like that barman up there who walked out into the center of the road with two pistols. Hell, he'd have been a sitting duck." London rocked forward and arose. "Speaking of barmen," he said, and stepped to the door.

They walked out, stood a moment in the settling dusk, looking both ways, then trooped on across the road and northward up to the Trail.

The place was jammed with men. The card tables were full and up at the bar men stood elbow to elbow. The only topic of conversation was what had occurred in the roadway shortly before sundown. When

Bellanger and London walked in, several half-smoked characters raised their unsteady glasses in toasts, and drank. The men were congenial in the Trail. They didn't push themselves on Bellanger and London; that wasn't the way of range men. But their admiration and respect were obvious in dozens of other ways.

Elmer Beadle brought two glasses and a bottle. He set them down and said drinks for Bellanger and London — who he called Landon — were on the house. He also told them he was the man who'd whistled earlier, to pass along the warnings. They invited Elmer to stay and have one with them. Beadle obliged but, after that, thumping fists atop his bar and stamping feet elsewhere took him hurriedly away.

The saloon was noisy, but in a subdued way. The smoke was thick enough to carve with a knife, and except for that powerful tobacco odor, the smell of horse sweat and man sweat would have predominated.

Sam Chavez came in, blinking. It was bright inside and dark outside. Several men who recalled Sam's part in the showdown saw him and called a rough welcome. Old Sam grinned, then made his way across to where Lou and Jim were leaning. He said — "You come with me." — and kept on grinning, but his light eyes weren't smiling at all. Lou straightened off the bar. So did Jim. In their business a smile meant nothing unless it was followed by smiling words. Chavez might look one way, but his words sounded very definitely another way. They put aside their glasses and turned to work their way back through the mob to the roadside doorway. Right after they passed through, Lou reached out.

"What is it, Sam?"

"The Hudsons," Chavez said. "We'll talk later."

The three men walked through late evening, southward. When Chavez reached the intersecting roadway leading westerly, which was the same roadway that old cotton-topped character with the buffalo carbine had disappeared down after the earlier face down, he turned and briskly walked as far as the fourth house down that gloomy little side road, and there Jamie was standing outside in a weed patch lawn with the same old man who'd had the buffalo gun. Jamie's gaze was milky; his lips were wet and pouting. When Jim and Lou walked up with Sam Chavez, Jamie looked straight through them. From inside the house a woman's thin wail sounded. Lou turned on Chavez. "What is it?" he asked.

"Their children," replied the old man standing out there with Jamie in the thin moonlight. "Their children have gone."

"Gone? Gone where?"

Chavez kept watching the older man. When he seemed unable to say any more, Sam spoke out. "The kids were playing outside. That's all anyone knows. They'd been playin' outside most of the evening after bein' cooped up in the house most of the day. A little while back, when Judith Hudson went lookin' for them at suppertime, they weren't around. I was walking past out yonder. She asked me if I'd seen them. I joined in the search." Sam paused, looked at Jamie and the distraught white-haired man, then he said in a lower tone: "There are horse tracks over in the back alley. It's

152

too dark now, but in daylight you can read them easily enough."

"All right," snapped Jim London. "What did they say, Chavez?"

"Three riders. One stayed in the saddle. The other two got down and stood looking through knotholes in the backyard fence, right into this yard." Chavez paused. "It was dusk. I couldn't make out much more except that one of those dismounted men came into the yard. After that, I couldn't tell. But in daylight . . ."

"In daylight," said Lou coldly, "those kids could be thirty miles from here, or . . ."

That wail came thinly from the interior of the house again. The white-haired man said: "Judith. It hit her almighty hard."

London turned away from the others and looked at Lou Bellanger's night-shadowed, hat-brim-hidden, bronzed face. "He wouldn't do that," Jim said, not very convincingly. "Hell, he wouldn't do a stinkin' lousy thing like that."

Bellanger thought differently. "A man who'll have a man bushwhacked, and who'll have another man beat over the head until he's childish, sure as hell would do a thing like this, Jim. I think I've had about enough, too."

"Hold it," London said quickly, when Lou turned. "Hold it. This isn't any private feud, Lou." London hesitated, but only briefly. He turned and said to Chavez: "Stay with these folks. Maybe you'd better get Doc Hart over here." Then he hastened on out through the gate into the roadway where Lou Bellanger was stiffly standing. Together, they hiked swiftly back up toward the main thoroughfare. When they came out opposite the jailhouse, Jim said: "Listen, Lou, it might not even be Mexican Hat. It might be someone else."

"You know better'n that," gritted Bellanger, coming to a hard halt. "No one else would have any reason. The Hudsons have no money. Who'd hold two kids for ransom unless he knew exactly what it was the Hudsons had that he wanted?"

London couldn't argue with that, so he said: "We'll go get a posse and ride out there."

But Bellanger shook his head. "I'm goin' out there right now, Jim. You can do whatever you want . . . fetch a posse or not . . . but I'm on my way now."

"Sure," said London sarcastically. "It's dark. You don't know the country out toward Mexican Hat that well, but Shafter's men do know it. You said it yourself a while back . . . a man who'd bushwhack would do just about anything. Lou, if he took those kids to force the Hudsons to sign his lousy quitclaim deed, believe me he'll be waitin' for someone to come out there. He'll be waitin' with guns all around."

Bellanger put a slow, speculative gaze upon Jim London. "You're talkin' like someone who wants Shafter to win," he said.

For a second London's odd-colored eyes flashed, then the mood passed, and he said quietly, almost frostily: "All I want is to end this thing right, Lou. We can't do it gettin' killed in some lousy ambush by a bunch of two-bit cowboys. If he has the kids, we'll get

154

them back. Don't you ever doubt that. But you're goin' about this like some emotional damned fool, an' you know as well as I do that fellers in our line of work never act like that. The minute we do, we wind up dead."

Bellanger was being held back, being made to talk out his explosive rush of white-hot feeling against the abduction of his mother's children. Whether Jim had meant it to be this way or not, that's how it eventually worked out. Lou slumped, stepped over to the edge of the plank walk, and started to make a smoke. Northward, up at the Trail, someone had started singing, but elsewhere, except for window lights here and there, the town was quiet and dark. Dr. Hart crossed the roadway up there with a shorter man beside him. It was too dark to identify the other man, but Lou knew it would be Sam Chavez. Sam led Hart down between two buildings in a short cut and after that the roadway was empty for a while.

Jim held the match for Lou. Bellanger inhaled, exhaled, and looked down. "You're right," he mumbled. "All right, Jim. Let's go get the posse."

But London didn't agree to that now, although earlier he'd made the suggestion. Instead, he stood in the shadows gazing down toward the livery barn as though turning some new notion over and over in his mind. In the end he said: "Lou, Shafter's goin' to show his hand before long, if he's the one."

"What do you mean if? You know damned well he's the one!"

"All right. But he's still goin' to show his hand. He's got to. What good are a couple of little kids to a man like Lacey Shafter?"

"No good at all . . . unless he's blind mad over what we did to him out in the roadway today. In that case I wouldn't bet money one way or another on what he'd do."

A horseman came riding down the northward roadway. Neither London nor Bellanger had seen him when he first came into view so they had no idea whether he came from up by the Trail, or whether he'd just arrived in town and was coming southward toward the livery barn. They didn't pay much attention to him in either case, until he came through the light up by the saloon, then Lou said: "Hell, that's Sam Chavez. I thought he was down with the Hudsons." They watched Chavez coming toward them, puzzled. Actually there wasn't anything too difficult to understand. Chavez owned a horse, he'd had plenty of time to take Dr. Hart down to the place where the Hudsons were staying, and afterward go get his animal and ride out. It was simply that neither London nor Bellanger had thought Chavez would be doing that, so, when the saddle maker came down closer, Lou stepped out beyond the overhang where moonlight fell across him. Jim stood upon the plank walk's edge behind Lou and to one side of him.

Chavez saw them and reined over. He was solemn when he halted and gazed downward. "I figured you'd still be in town," he said. "I was at the livery barn." He leaned down, holding something out. Lou took it and Jim London moved in closer also to see. Chavez said:

156

"He wouldn't have done that with Bob Nichol. He wouldn't have tried it at all. But he knows something, I think, about you two, so there it is."

Chavez was referring to the slip of paper he'd handed Lou Bellanger. It was a simple note with the words scrawled in heavy pencil saying that the Hudson children wouldn't be harmed providing Bellanger and London released the men from jail they'd locked in there this afternoon, and providing London and Bellanger left the country by noon the following day. If those terms were met, the Hudson children would be restored to their parents the next day, unharmed. It was also implied that, unless those terms were met, the children might never see their parents again.

London swore and Sam Chavez nodded agreement with each blistering oath.

Lou folded the paper and handed it back to Sam. "Go on back," he said. "Tell the folks we'll set the gunmen loose, an' we'll pull out of Brigham, come sunup."

Chavez nodded, his steely, grave eyes puckered. "But you have something in mind," he said.

Lou considered the saddle maker. Chavez had proved himself time and time again. Still, the fewer people who knew something, the fewer slips there could inadvertently be. "Just go on back, Sam, and tell the Hudsons we'll agree to Shafter's terms. *Adiós*."

Sam gravely nodded and reined away. "*Adiós*," he said quietly. "And good luck."

CHAPTER
FOURTEEN

Jim didn't ask what was in Bellanger's mind, which was probably just as well since Lou didn't have it perfected anyway. But, with this fresh shift of the wind, they didn't head for either the Trail to get posse men, or down to the livery barn after their horses. Instead, they walked over in front of the jailhouse, Lou still smoking his cigarette, Jim not smoking but equally as grave and thoughtful.

"We let 'em out," said Lou. "But first let's do a little doctoring on guns and gun belts."

They went inside, closed the door, and took down the guns of their three prisoners. "Forgot to get their shell belts, too," Lou said. "Well, it doesn't matter. Is there a file around here?"

Jim didn't know, so they looked. There were several files, in fact, in a box of small hand tools. "Just a quarter inch ought to do it," said Lou, sitting down and cocking the pistol in his hand.

"More than a quarter inch," corrected Jim London. "I've done this before. You got to take it down so's the firin' pin drops into its hole all right, but doesn't quite go all the way through. Then you got to file the cussed things sharp again so, if a feller happens to check them, they'll look just like they're supposed to look."

While they worked, they talked a little, making a plan, revising it, perfecting it, and, when they had the three six-guns rendered completely useless, they'd finished making their plan, too.

Jim arose, took the keys, and went over to the cell-room door. He turned to make certain the weapons looked perfectly normal where they were hanging from wall pegs, then he solemnly winked, and Lou just as solemnly winked back.

The three gunfighters were puffy-eyed. They'd been asleep. The wounded Mexican Hat cowboy sat up, looking much better and asked when London would release him. All Jim did was wither the cowboy with a look, say nothing to him, and herd the three gunfighters out into the office. He closed the door, leaned upon it, and said: "I'm goin' to turn you boys loose."

The gunfighters looked pleased. They also looked mildly bewildered, but they sat, saying nothing. Lou Bellanger had his hat tipped low so the lamplight wouldn't reach his narrow eyes.

"You're goin' to get a little advice," he said softly, bringing the attention of the gunfighters around. "Don't go out to Mexican Hat." He then explained about the abduction, about the terms Lacey Shafter had laid down. He concluded with: "It's not just a matter of Shafter trying to steal land any more, boys. It goes a lot deeper than that. If you go out there, you're likely to end up dead. So is Shafter and you can tell him that for me, because maybe he won this round, but we'll be back someday to settle with him."

"Someday . . . ?" murmured the youth called Boyd. "What does that mean, Bellanger?"

"It means that Jim and I are leaving town. Those were the rest of Shafter's terms. We set you boys free, then we leave the country, and he'll send the kids back to their folks. We'll leave like he wants, an' we're settin' you fellers free. But Lacey Shafter's makin' a bad mistake if he thinks we'll stay away forever. You tell him that, if you go out there, but remember what I said. You'll likely wind up dead if you go."

Jim crossed to the wall pegs, took down those three six-guns, went over, and tossed each man one of the guns. Then he went across to the door and threw it open. It was dark out, and turning quiet up and down the roadway. The gunfighters switched weapons until each man had his own gun, and then they arose, eager to leave.

The youngest one paused and said: "That wounded feller in there. He confirmed it. You're sure 'nough Two-Gun Jim London. What in hell are you doin', wearin' a lawman's badge?"

Jim jerked his head coldly. "Out," he ordered, and, when the youth moved past and paused upon the yonder plank walk, Jim said: "You got some real good advice a minute ago. Be smart, fellers, take it."

He stood there with the lamplight behind him, watching them. When they continued to hesitate, he told them their horses were down at the livery barn.

160

That gave them a course to follow, so they finally moved out, walking with sudden purpose in the night.

Lou came over to step outside and watch. "They'll be at Mexican Hat for breakfast," he dourly prophesied. "The damned fools." Jim stepped back inside for his hat and to blow out the lamp, then he and Lou also started down toward the livery barn. As they passed the saddle shop, a mahogany old leathery face was back in shadows, watching them walk past.

The gunfighters were gone. As the night hawk said, looking troubled: "I figured they'd escaped, Sheriff. I was wonderin' whether I ought to try an' get the shotgun from the harness room or not. Then they said they'd been released. But they sure lost no time in riggin' out and gettin' away from here."

"Which way did they ride?" Jim asked. "South or northwest?"

"Northwest."

Jim threw a cynical look at Lou, and they also went after their horses. With the night hawk moving around to help, Lou said: "Well, it's been an interestin' stay in your town, friend."

The night hawk straightened up, baffled. "You mean you fellers are pullin' out, too?"

London, rising up to settle across his saddle, nodded downward. He didn't offer any explanation. His face was set in a hard, tough expression, and that discouraged the bewildered night hawk from asking any more questions.

They left the livery barn riding side by side, heading straight southward. The liveryman back there went out as far as the roadway to look after them, scratching his head. When he returned to the barn, he looked deeply upset about something. It wasn't difficult to sense his dilemma if those two men were abandoning his town, for the liveryman and everyone else who'd been involved in that earlier showdown with Mexican Hat the real trouble was just beginning.

But Lou and Jim went southward only as far as it was necessary to lose sight of the town, which meant that no one back there could see them, either. Then they swung off to the right and raised a lope that they held their mounts to for a half hour before slowing again. They were by this time well north and west of Brigham, over on Hudson range. They talked little. Men in their line of work knew instinctively what things to do in almost any given situation. There were, of course, many alternatives, but Jim London and Lou Bellanger, while they'd never worked together before, nor even met before for that matter, thought very much alike under stress. It was for this reason they didn't have to do a lot of talking.

Their plan was very simple. Spy on the headquarters ranch of Mexican Hat, and, when the men rode down to Brigham to release the Hudson children, get in behind them and trail them, because it was, as Lou had pointed out back in the jailhouse when they'd been perfecting this plan, certainly not Lacey Shafter's intention simply to hand over the children without also demanding that Judith and Jamie Hudson sign the quitclaim to their land.

Lou knew about where Mexican Hat's headquarters were, but Jim knew the way. He'd already been there, but that had been in the daylight. They lost a little time, therefore, finding the place, but when at last they rode up over a land swell and saw lights not more than a mile ahead, they knew they had arrived. It was close to midnight now. Cowmen ordinarily retired very early — unless, like Shafter down there, they had some very excellent reason for sitting up half the night.

"Quite a set-up," observed Jim London. "You know, Lou, years back I was the range boss of an outfit as big as this."

Lou hadn't known that. "If you'd stayed with it," he retorted, "by now you'd be able to bed down nice and peaceful every night."

Jim made a crooked smile. "Sure. That's what cattle do. Bed down every night. Me, I'm hooked up wrong for that kind of a life. And so are you. Our kind, well, we just keep headin' into the sunsets until we run out of time. For me an' you it's a far better way of life."

Lou considered London. "There've been times when I haven't been convinced you really believe that, Jim. In the office tonight, for instance, when Burgess and those other town fathers came in to call us local heroes . . ."

Jim had no answer. He sat his horse gazing down at that sprawl of log buildings, his face wiped clean of all expression. After a while he said: "Let's go. The gunfighters ought to be inside by now, havin' a drink and tellin' Shafter and his boys how we set them loose, then rode on out like he said for us to do."

They left the low hill, circling far around to come in behind the buildings. There was a lighted bunkhouse up there, a lighted main house, and off to one side of the owner's residence a lighted cook shack. What Lou and Jim were careful of was the way the breeze might come this late at night. They had no wish to be disclosed by nickering horses or a barking dog.

It was a long wait. The night turned cold. They put on jackets, squatted in front of their patient horses, and kept their long vigil. Once, Lou cussed because it was too risky to light a smoke. Another time Jim London stood up to kick some pins and needles out of a sleeping foot. He stamped around a moment, then knelt upon one knee, gazing over where the cook shack light was extinguished.

"They'll either hit the sack," he grumbled, "or hit the trail. I wonder if they've got those little kids in the bunkhouse?"

"Main house more'n likely," stated Lou. "You know, the more I think on it, the more I believe Lacey Shafter's a little on the light side upstairs. Even if the Hudsons sign his quitclaim deed, it wouldn't hold up in court, and I've a hunch even Jamie'll go to bat the minute he gets his kids back."

Jim London turned a sardonic look at his companion. "You're dreaming," he said. "Lou, after Shafter gets their signatures on that quitclaim, what makes you think they're going to be alive?"

Bellanger kept staring over at those buildings for a moment after London said that. Then he slowly turned his night-shadowed face and the blueness of his eyes

164

was like the deep-down color of ice. He didn't say a word and neither did Jim, for a while, but eventually London added one more sentence to what he'd already said.

"That's why this was done at night."

Lou stood up, bending his knees to restore impaired circulation. "I didn't figure the thing through," he muttered. "I reckon when a feller's too involved, like you've already said, he's not as coldly practical as he needs to be."

"That's dead right!" exclaimed London. "Look, Shafter's not as light in the head as you think he is. He knew exactly what he was doing, grabbin' those little kids after nightfall. He'll take 'em back . . . not tomorrow . . . but tonight. Who'll see him? No one who could swear in the darkness it was definitely Lacey Shafter. He'll hand over the kids after the Hudsons sign the quitclaim. After that, it'll be several hours before sunup when folks are around again for the Hudsons to tell their story, too. By then . . ." London gave his thin shoulder a rough heave up and down. "Maybe it'll be an accident. Like a runaway or something. Accidental death, Lou, and the land belongs to Mexican Hat. Maybe I'm guessin' wild, but I recollect a case like this before, up in Montana."

"They're comin' out," said Lou, standing very stiffly, and straining to see over there into the ranch yard. "Watch the light in front of the main house. You'll see 'em moving across it toward the barn."

Jim saw them, but he couldn't determine how many men were over there. The last man, however, came forth with a lantern, and that helped. There seemed to be four men, not counting the one with the lantern.

Lou stepped back beside his horse and waited. He was ice-cold in the face. Jim saw that and it pleased him. He by far preferred having a man whose blood was ice water at his side when there might be trouble, than someone likely to explode with emotion.

The Mexican Hat riders rigged out by lantern light in the barn, then led forth their horses, and climbed aboard. For a moment or two afterward there was a little fidgeting, but because the lantern was still hanging inside the barn neither Lou nor Jim could determine the cause for this. All the same Lou made a close guess.

"Takin' the kids up behind their saddles."

The moment the Mexican Hat riders started out of the yard, Lou and Jim also mounted up and started moving. It wasn't difficult to keep the men in front of them in view, and even once or twice, when the Mexican Hat riders passed around low hills, they could still keep track of them by their rattling rein chains and squeaking leather.

Lou studied the position of the thin moon and said he thought it had to be about one o'clock in the morning. He also said that this would put Shafter and his men into Brigham about two-thirty or three o'clock, which would be just about the right time, if Jim's notion of how Shafter meant to work it was right.

"Not even very many dogs are awake at three in the morning."

The Mexican Hat riders weren't pushing their horses. When they were close enough to town to catch the first scents coming back from the place, three riders peeled off and loped ahead.

Jim grunted about that. "Those lousy gunfighters," he said. "Well, they asked for it. Can't say they didn't get plenty of good advice."

The town loomed up ahead, a jumble of square houses, buildings, and little outhouse sheds. There was a visible light down at the livery barn, but elsewhere the place looked totally dark. Shafter's gunfighters returned and led the rest of the riders around town to the north, then dropped southward, which was precisely the correct route to take to reach the little house where the Hudsons were staying.

Lou and Jim turned off behind Beadle's saloon, took their carbines, and left their horses tied to a rickety fence. As they started ahead on foot, a dirty cloud floated over the face of the moon, making the night even darker.

CHAPTER
FIFTEEN

They reached a corner of the alleyway leading down
behind that house where Judith and Jamie were staying,
and saw horsemen. The distance was something like
300 or 400 feet, so it was impossible to make out much
more than shapes of mounted men, but it was enough,
since they already knew who'd be down there.

They discussed waiting until Shafter went inside with
the children, then jumping the others, but Jim was
against that on the grounds that it might get the wrong
people hurt if everyone started shooting anywhere near
the house.

A light in the back room of the house yonder was
lifted and moved. Someone was admitted through the
back door. Just for a moment, while lamplight outlined
the shapes on the porch, Lou and Jim London saw
three silhouettes. One of them, they were certain, had
to be Lacey Shafter, but the other two could have come
out of the house; it was too far for the men on foot to
be certain.

Lou stepped back and pressed his back into a fence.
"As near as I can make out, Shafter and maybe one
other man went up to the house. That leaves maybe
another four or five down the alley. It's too damned

168

dark to tell for sure. They're sittin' all together down there. You want to take on those odds?"

Jim nodded. "Sure. But not until they come up the alleyway toward us."

They waited, and meanwhile the moon crept from behind that dirty old cloud, floated briefly across a pale sky, then plunged into another, even larger and thicker cloud. Lou cursed under his breath.

A dog started barking beyond the fence where Lou and Jim stood. That started other dogs barking throughout town. Lou might have worried except that the horsemen down the dark alleyway paid no attention to the barking. Probably because they considered themselves to be the cause of it.

Jim looked out and around. The light down yonder had moved ahead in the house, as though someone had carried it into the front parlor perhaps. Jim drew back. "They've got their kids back," he surmised. "They'll be handin' over the land."

Lou said nothing. He drew forth his six-gun, held it up close to his face, and carefully inspected it. Jim watched this, then tartly said: "No one ever files off the firin' pin on his own gun, not even by mistake."

The waiting was hard. They had no idea what was going on inside that little house. The only consolation was the fact that Shafter had no real reason to pistol-whip any of those people, plus the fact that he'd wish for silence.

Then one of the horsemen climbed down and went over into the yard, and that aroused the curiosity of both watchers until they saw a man walk forth from the shadows up by the rear door, followed after a little interval by a second man. This second one was carrying two rifles, or what looked to be rifles. As he crossed toward the alleyway, he flung the rifles into a geranium bed.

"Disarmed 'em inside the house," Jim said. "They'll be coming now, Lou."

The horsemen were getting impatient. One of them called roughly ahead in a subdued voice. That fat cloud passed, and the moon jumped out into a clear stretch of heaven again. The light increased a little, but it was still a dark night. That moon up there was little more than a sharp-pointed crescent.

The horsemen mounted and turned, heading westerly up the alleyway straight toward Lou Bellanger and Jim London. They slouched along suspecting nothing. They rode close to one another, making it all the more difficult to determine their numbers or to pick out Lacey Shafter. When they were only 100 or so feet away, Lou stepped up to the corner of the fence. Jim was off a little distance to Lou's left, and Jim dropped down to one knee the way a rifleman might have taken his fighting position, but neither Lou nor Jim was using their carbines. They'd propped those guns upon the fence and had their six-guns up and ready.

One of the riders suddenly halted and turned in the saddle. "Hey," he said softly yet insistently. "Put that woman up here in front. Mister Shafter, if them fellers just ducked around, then come back to town like you said they might do, they could be waitin' up here somewhere for us, so put the woman out front an' that'll keep 'em from shootin'."

Lou stiffened. Twenty feet away Jim London jumped up and sprinted swiftly over to get into the darkness by the fence. He had heard those words the same as Lou had, and Jim was a quick-witted man. He knew, also, that the woman that Mexican Hat cowboy had to be talking about was either the white-thatched old man's wife from back at the little house, or else it had to be Judith Hudson, but in either event Jim knew he and Lou didn't dare fire as long as there was any danger at all of hitting her.

Lou stepped back one big stride, grabbed Jim's gun wrist, and pulled. They ran back alongside the fence a full 100 feet before Lou halted and released London. He was breathing hard. Jim flexed his fingers, holstered his six-gun, and whispered: "Maybe I was wrong. Maybe they don't aim to have an accident happen to your ma or Jamie, after all. Maybe they're just goin' to hold your ma to make certain Jamie and those other folks back there keep quiet."

"The reason doesn't matter," hissed Lou. "They've got her along and we don't dare shoot. Come on."

"Where?"

"Back to the horses to trail them. What else can we do, except hope and pray for a better time? Come on."

Taking their carbines with them, they trotted back to the rickety fence where they'd left their horses tied, got astride, and turned to go softly back down toward the place where they'd last seen Shafter and his riders. When they arrived there, the other men were gone. Lou turned out into the alleyway and slowly walked his horse in the same direction his enemies had also gone. Jim kept up beside him, but Jim was troubled. He hadn't anticipated this at all. As far as Jim London was concerned, he'd figured to end the entire affair back there in a blaze of roaring guns.

Up ahead, where the alleyway ended and Brigham's main east-west thoroughfare passed along, the light was a little better, but not much. They caught one fleeting glimpse of the men from Mexican Hat, turning right up the road in the general direction of the Trail Saloon, which also happened to be the way out of town, after they'd made one more bend around an intersecting roadway.

By the time Lou and Jim got up where they'd risk a look, Shafter's men had already taken that intersecting roadway, heading back upon the open range. Jim said — "Now." — and urged his horse ahead. "Follow me," he said to Lou, and didn't follow the Mexican Hat riders at all, but cut straight across the road, passed over an empty lot between two stores, and kept right on going until he was through Brigham and on the yonder range, and that was when the moon jumped out again, flooding the dark land with a pallid, wet-seeming light.

Lou hissed and pointed. The men with Lacey Shafter were riding swiftly now, heading due west instead of north-west. Jim reined down and rubbed his jaw about this. "We don't even know if they've still got her. For that matter, Lou, we don't even know who *she* is."

172

Lou pointed in the direction the riders were passing down the gloomy night. "We know, all right," he said. "Who else would they be takin' to the Hudson Ranch?"

After that the pair of them resumed their trailing, always well back, always choosing their footing so as to make no noise. That was a help, but as it turned out being so silent also happened to betray them. At least it partially betrayed them, because when they approached that intersecting hill, which cut off the sight of the Hudson place, they slowed to a scant walk and came around the south flank of the low ridge and almost rode right up on top of a mounted man who was off his horse, standing there, looking ahead where the others were continuing on down toward the buildings.

There wasn't time to shoot; they came upon this straggler too suddenly. Lou's horse took several forward-thrusting steps around the hill, treading on springtime grass, and there the dismounted man was, his back to them. Lou dropped both reins and lunged. The stranger turned, finally, at the sibilant sound of leather rubbing over leather. He caught Lou head-on.

They fell and rolled, the stranger striving frantically to pull his gun and Lou striving just as powerfully to prevent the gun from being drawn. Jim London couldn't help right away. He had to jump ahead and catch Lou's astonished horse before the animal ran on down where Shafter and the balance of his Mexican Hat riders were approaching the Hudson ranch yard.

The man beneath Lou was strong and solid. It was a weird fight because each man could only use one fist. Their other hands were locked over that gun in the stranger's holster. Lou tried to catch his arching, twisting adversary under the jaw, and missed. He tried hammering the man's face and only connected once, while at the same time the cowboy struck him hard in the middle.

The cowboy rolled, seeking to throw Lou off. That failed, so he tried to yell out for the others to come back, and Lou stopped that with a hard strike to the side of the cowboy's head that made the man groggy. He raised up, caught Lou around the neck, and pressed his head close to avoid being struck alongside the head again.

That seemed to turn the tide, though. The cowboy's reflexes were slower after being sledged up beside the head. He hung on, and that also incapacitated his free hand, but it didn't do much more than make Lou's blows land closer in and lower down. He hammered repeatedly at his adversary's middle.

In desperation the man from Mexican Hat released the pistol he'd been trying to draw, wrenched violently sideways to get away from those punishing strikes in the middle, and broke loose. He rolled once, got both legs gathered, and sprang upright. Lou did the same, ten feet away, but slower. The cowboy turned, aimed a savage kick, and let fly. Lou threw up an arm, felt boot leather grate over bone and muscle, and gritted his teeth against the pain. Then he, too, was on his feet.

The cowboy rushed him. Lou probably should have given ground, but he didn't. He leaned into that battering ram charge and swung fiercely the moment the stranger was close enough. The shock of a solid

174

blow traveled all the way to Lou's shoulder, but the other man was heavier. Lou was knocked off balance. It didn't matter; the cowboy was reeling. That blow had hurt him badly. He pawed Lou off with extended hands, but most of the fight was knocked out of him.

Lou moved in on the stranger, caught him high on the shoulder, making him loosen still more, then he cocked his right fist. A quiet, clipped voice said: "Don't wreck him. We need to hear some answers."

Lou slowly eased off. Jim walked on up, put forth a hand, and caught the staggering cowboy, eased him down gently, and knelt down beside him, at the same time gazing upward. "Man, you're sure vindictive," he said to Lou. "All you've got to do with 'em is knock 'em silly. You don't have to batter their brains out."

Lou dropped both arms and stood, wide-legged, while he sucked in greedy amounts of fresh night air. It hadn't been much of a battle actually, but a man puts just as much effort into a short fight as a long one.

Jim steadied their captive and lightly slapped the man's face. That cowboy, though, had taken a lot of hard blows. He was a long time coming around. Jim finally thumbed back his hat, made himself comfortable on the grass, and waited. Lou went over where their horses patiently stood, tied to a skimpy sage bush, and dug in one of his saddlebags for a bandanna to wipe sweat off. When he finally had his wind and returned, the cowboy was beginning to squint his eyes, then jumped them wide open, evidently trying to clear his foggy vision. The minute Lou walked up and the cowboy saw him, he dived for his hip holster again. Jim

175

London held up the man's six-gun in plain sight, then tossed it over one shoulder out into the grass.

"Now, then," Jim said. "Who's the lady Shafter has with him?"

The cowboy put a hand to his split lips, saw blood, and fished out a soiled handkerchief to dab at the wound. He looked from Jim to Lou and back again, not offering a word.

Jim sighed, stood up, and said: "Lou, maybe if you loosened some teeth, or maybe broke his nose, he'd feel more like talkin'."

Lou took one step forward, and the cowboy spoke swiftly. "It's Miz Hudson."

"What does Shafter figure to do with her down there at the ranch?" asked Jim.

The cowboy shrugged. "I don't know. Mister Shafter don't have to tell us everything he does."

Lou bent, caught the cowboy's shirt, and lifted the man off the ground one-handed. The cowboy was not a small man. Lou pulled him in very close. "One more try," he said. "And if you don't know the answer . . . I'm going to kill you. Why Missus Hudson?"

"Leggo, dammit, you're chokin' me. Because Lacey said we got to keep her to be sure them other folks back there in that house don't tell no one what's happened."

"And if they do tell, then what?"

"How would I know? Lacey didn't say. But I can guess, Bellanger, an' so can you. He'll shoot her. He's got to get rid of them Hudsons anyway."

Lou swung. When the blow connected, it sounded like a small-caliber revolver being fired. The cowboy's

176

head went violently backward, his knees buckled, and Lou let him fall.

Jim helped bind and gag the man, then they went to their horses. There Lou said: "We've got to do it without a sound, Jim. One gunshot and he just might go ahead and shoot her. You ready?"

They got astride, cast a final look at the wreckage of Shafter's cowboy, and headed down toward the buildings, where someone had a lamp going in the late and dismal night. Everywhere else, there was only darkness. They used that light to set their course by, and headed around toward the south.

CHAPTER
SIXTEEN

They had one distinct advantage: the men from Mexican Hat had no idea Bellanger and London were so close. From what they'd heard one of the men say back in town, Shafter evidently hadn't been convinced they'd leave town and not return. But out here at the Hudson place it was reasonably safe to assume Shafter wasn't worried about them now, because they hadn't shown up in town, after all.

Where they halted out in the southward night, there was a widespread consultation. The decision was to go up as far as they dared, hide their horses, then go the balance of the way on foot. Beyond that they made no plan. As Lou said, there was no way under the sun — or moon — to guess what they might encounter, so they'd meet each situation as it arose.

There was a little shallow erosion gully not far ahead. It wasn't deep enough to hide horses. In fact, it was scarcely deep enough to hide two prone men, but several sturdy trees grew in it, and that's where they rode up, tied their horses, and crept forward again, but this time on foot. They'd decided to leave their carbines back there. Whatever occurred up in the yard was going to be well within the limits of six-gun range.

178

They used the light to set their onward course by. When they got close enough to make out buildings, Jim said they should go around to the barn and, if possible, if the horses weren't guarded over there, set the men from Mexican Hat afoot by running off their mounts. After that, Jim pointed out, Lacey Shafter couldn't send for help, if it turned out that he might need it.

Lou turned a sardonic grin upon his companion. "If Shafter needs help," he said. "With odds against us somethin' like three to one, Jim, I don't think he's too likely to need it. But all right, let's go."

They had to go out and around to get down beyond the main house to the barn, but they made it without difficulty. Where they encountered the first trouble was at the corral out back where the Hudsons' horses were. A couple of cowboys were leaning upon the corral back there, looking in at the horses and idly discussing their merits and demerits. One of them said: "You'd think them folks would've had enough sense to keep their best horses corralled, not these jug-headed critters."

His companion made a more revealing comment. "They didn't get no chance. By the time they figured someone was makin' off with their livestock, what was left?"

The first cowboy chuckled. "I reckon you're right at that. Well, they had a pretty fair team, only they never turned 'em out, otherwise somebody'd have picked up a few dollars on them, too."

The talk went on. The cowboys stood, relaxed and comfortable, over there in the balmy night between Lou and Jim, and the rear entrance to the barn, until

London shook his head in exasperation and whispered that those two obviously had been left to guard the horses in the barn, and the only way they were going to get past them was to do as they'd done to that other one they'd met back over by the eastward hill.

There was nothing wrong with this except that, between the barn and where London and Bellanger crouched, there wasn't a tree, a bush, or even a decent-size dung pile out back of the barn.

Those two cowboys up there turned their backs on the corralled horses and leaned there, desultorily talking, smoking, and occasionally yawning. Jim straightened up, making a careful study of them. Finally he said in a bare whisper: "You try getting over by the corrals. I'm goin' to start whistling and walking over to them. While they're watchin' me, you get close enough to get the drop on 'em."

Jim walked away, on an angling course that left the impression he'd come around behind the barn from the direction of the main house. He began by humming the tune "Shenandoah", and eventually he began to whistle the same music softly.

Lou held his breath while the pair of cowboys turned, not especially alarmed but strongly curious as they watched Jim approaching them. One of them dropped his smoke and stamped on it. The other one stood watching, his entire attention focused upon London. That was Lou's cue. He began a careful, sidling walk forward, but in such a way that it took him squarely around behind the watching pair, and led him in toward the corral.

180

He crossed the open place handily and began angling toward the corral. Up ahead, Jim London was ambling along at a reduced gait, for while he and the pair of range men were facing one another, Jim could see past them, past the corral and out where Lou was moving up wraith-like, through the gloom. Jim was adjusting his forward progress to Lou's stealthy, slow advance.

One of the cowboys said: "That you, Jack? What's new up at the house?"

Jim tried to time his answer and at the same time slur his words. He wasn't more than fifty or sixty feet away when he muttered one word: "Nothin'."

If the cowboys felt a foreign presence, they didn't give any immediate sign of it, but neither did either one of them speak again. Jim would very shortly now be within their sight, head-on. Lou saw this and took two more large steps forward to reach the corral. He stepped upon a dry twig. The stick snapped with a brittle, sharp report. Both the cowboys swung to see. Jim London jumped ahead and went for his gun. Lou froze, ducking low in the hope they wouldn't see him, but he had nothing more than pole-corral stringers to shield him, and, of course, they made out his lighter form against the darker landscape.

"Hold it!" growled Jim. "Stand steady, boys, you're covered!"

Both cowboys had their right hands straight down. Jim's lethal warning was all that kept them from blowing the silent night apart with gunfire. They turned a little, bodies stiff, to look back. Jim was only twenty feet off now and had his six-gun pointed straight at them.

The fight didn't go out of those two right away. They didn't say a word, didn't even shuffle their feet, or rub shoulders over the corral stringers at their back. They stood poised and wire-tight, almost, but not quite, willing to offer battle. They were tough men, not easily cowed or frightened. Jim could easily see how this entire confrontation hung by a hair, so he said: "Lou, get their guns!"

Bellanger moved swiftly along the west side of the corral. Inside, several horses indifferently watched what was going on with no inkling at all that it was trouble. Over at the house the silence hung as heavily as ever. Only in this one small area was there a roiled atmosphere of peril.

Lou was no more than thirty feet away and coming in behind the two captives when over against the eastward night a gunshot rang out. The sound echoed and rolled, sending slamming reverberations up and down the high vault of heaven. After a little interval, another gunshot rang out.

Both the cowboys as well as Lou Bellanger and Jim London were whipped out of their thralldom. The cowboys dropped, whirled, and lunged in opposite directions, going for their guns.

Lou beat them both to the draw very handily, but he had four rows of corral stringers interfering with his aim, so he dropped straight down and rolled, unable to fire his own gun and wishing to get away swiftly from where he had been so, when the cowboys fired, they wouldn't have him in their sights.

Jim fired, though, first to the left, then to the right. Both were snapped-off shots with his gun swinging. Aside from that the cowboys were jumping clear and squatting low. Jim missed both times.

The cowboys opened up in reply, and finally Lou let go with a shot from beneath the lowest corral stringer. He plowed a dusty furrow along the top of the ground that set those heretofore drowsing horses into panicked snorts and bounds.

From over at the main house a man's rough voice called profanely down toward the barn, but whatever the words were, they got drowned out in the crash and thunder of gunfire.

Lou could no longer see Jim. Evidently London had run back a distance to be out of sight. When he began firing again, though, Lou could place his position, and began crawling backward away from the corral as the cries and sounds of running men crossing from the direction of the main house came into the short lulls between gunshots.

Lou didn't fire after he got clear of the corral. He concentrated on just getting away before those men, who were running toward the barn from out front, got close enough to join the pair of embattled cowboys.

There were no more gunshots from out across the eastward range. In fact, except for the area within several hundred feet of the barn in all directions, the night was as gloomy and empty as ever.

Shafter and the rest of his Mexican Hat men, though, began firing blindly as soon as they charged down through the barn to the back door. That was when Lou and Jim got in their best work, too, for those reckless men filled the doorway. Lou didn't aim; he simply pointed toward the opening and let fly. Jim, off to the north but circling around southward toward a juncture with Bellanger, also let fly in the general direction of that blackly cavernous opening. They got at least one hit because a man's high wail came through the rattle and flash of battle.

Jim was back there waiting, when Lou finally could turn and run without being seen, through the layers of night farther out upon the range.

"We got to get out of here," panted Jim. "Head for the horses!"

They had no time for other talk, for recrimination or even brief speculation about those two shots upcountry that had routed out their enemies and had come in the eleventh hour to upset their hopes.

Shafter's men found out very soon that whoever they'd been fighting with in the darkness was gone. Men shouted back and forth as they fanned out in an aggressive hunt. Some of them turned southward inevitably, and paced gingerly around behind the house, but these men didn't even get close. They were walking; Bellanger and London were running.

Someone back in the barn called authoritatively for the Mexican Hat men to come back. That was the last sound Jim and Lou heard that was distinguishable, but as they jumped down into the little arroyo to trot over and jerk loose their tied reins and mount up, Lou said: "That'll be Shafter. He'll come lookin' on horseback now."

Jim also rode up out of the arroyo, but when Lou turned eastward to flee, Jim said: "Wait a minute. Maybe we can give 'em a run for their damned money." He sat perfectly erect in his saddle, listening to the sounds coming from the ranch. When Lou reined up beside him, Jim said: "This is a pretty good place to fool 'em, right here."

"How?" demanded the other gunfighter.

"Make enough noise to let them hear us and come chargin' down here, then turn the horses loose, lie quiet in that arroyo, and pray like hell they follow our loose horses all the way back to the livery barn in town."

They didn't have a whole lot of time to make their decision. Mounted men could be heard charging out over the northward land. Lou said: "Were they ridable . . . those damned horses back there in the corral? I never got a good look at them."

"Yeah, they were saddle animals," responded Jim London. "But just barely, a bunch of knot-heads."

"Even a knot-head, as long as it has four legs and a strong back, will be better'n tryin' to get away from the ranch on foot, if they overtake our horses and find out what we've done . . . tricked them."

Jim grinned fleetingly, stepped off, tugged out his carbine, and led the way. They took their horses back over into the shadowy little arroyo and stood there amid the scrub trees with them, each holding his carbine, each with his heart irregularly pounding as

185

they listened to the fluting calls of mounted searchers coming downcountry, but spread far out as though the men from Mexican Hat had no very clear notion in which direction their enemies had fled.

Lou said: "Try an' get a count when they go past. I want to know if they left a guard back with Miz Hudson at the ranch."

Jim didn't answer. He was looking northward. Suddenly in a loud voice of feigned agony he said: "Give me a hand into the saddle, this damned ankle of mine's busted sure."

Those words had scarcely been uttered when two oncoming riders hauled back and bellowed triumphantly for the balance of Shafter's men to converge. "We found 'em! We got 'em down here a ways. Hurry up!"

Lou and Jim stood poised, gauging the sounds of riders running together up in the darkness. Lou said — "Now!" — and looped his reins around the saddle horn, slapped his horse hard on the rump, and jumped back as the astonished animal gave a tremendous leap forward. Jim's horse jumped past, also. Finding themselves free, the pair of horses turned off after jumping out of the arroyo, heading almost due eastward. They ran, loose and free, increasing their speed the minute those charging Mexican Hat riders heard them and gave full chase, bellowing at the top of their lungs and occasionally letting loose a wild gunshot.

Jim and Lou kneeled in among the saplings in their shallow place, listening to the chase. Once, a rider swerved out of the west, skirting their arroyo carefully, being careful where his mount stepped, then, upon the east side, hung in the hooks and went racing on, in the van of his excited companions. That was as close as any of those men came to meeting each other.

Jim stood up, unsmiling. Lou stood a moment longer, listening to those diminishing cries and ragged gunshots, then said: "Hell, with the devil behind them our horses will be doing good if they stop this side of the Utah line. Let's go."

They had something like a mile to walk over before getting within sight of the buildings again. There was still that lamp burning at the house. Off in the gray east there was another very faint kind of firming-up light, too. It meant that dawn wasn't far off. It was this, more than the possibility of the Mexican Hat men returning, that put a fresh spring into the steps of Bellanger and London as they came in closer behind the ranch house. Whatever they accomplished here would have to be concluded before daylight came; their only ally all night long had been the darkness. When that dissipated, they'd be clear targets to any Mexican Hat men who happened to spy them.

The yard was deathly still. There was a heavy scent of dust in the air; otherwise, the place seemed entirely abandoned.

CHAPTER
SEVENTEEN

They didn't go directly to the house, but back around toward the barn again, exactly as they'd done earlier. It proved a good precaution. There was a horse tied in a stall there, saddled and bridled, but the saddle boot was empty, which meant that whoever owned this beast had his Winchester with him.

Jim threw up his hands and nodded across the yard toward the house. "Well, he's ready, whoever he is. Let's go. We don't want to keep him waiting."

They didn't cross the yard, for an obvious reason, but instead went out back and down the southerly side of the buildings almost to the main house. Lou gestured. They would split up, one coming in from the west, one approaching the house from the east. It was the logical approach, but as it turned out it wasn't necessary.

A man opened the front door a crack, letting an oblong shaft of orange lamplight show, flipped a cigarette far out into the yard, and just for a moment stood peeking out. Lou and Jim froze, watching and waiting. The man opened the door a little wider, emboldened by the silence, and shoved his entire head out to look left and right. When he straightened up after that, he stood in plain sight, obviously lulled into a sense of security. He was a lanky individual, hatless and rough-looking. Neither Lou nor Jim knew him; at least, that far off and shadowed by the overhang roof of the Hudsons' porch, they didn't recognize him.

He turned finally, industriously scratching under his ribs, and looked into the parlor. Then he closed the door. Lou relaxed, letting out a long breath. "Just that one man," he said quietly, "and he's not very worried. Let's just go on over an' pay him a social call."

They sidled down to the west end of the porch, stepped up, testing the old planking, found it solid enough, and moved cautiously straight down toward the front door. Beyond the door was that solitary double-hung window where the lamplight fell outward across the porch into the dusty yonder yard.

When they were close enough, Lou ducked far down, scuttled over, and got on the far side of the window. From back there in gloom he could see inside. Opposite him, covering the door, Jim palmed his six-gun and waited.

Judith Hudson was sitting on a thin old sofa over near the rock fireplace. To Lou's surprise, instead of wringing her hands or weeping, she was impassively knitting. From time to time she'd raise her eyes and look at the slouching man across from her sitting in a rocking chair with his hat on the floor by his side and his Winchester carbine loosely held across his upper legs. Except for that carbine it would have been a homey scene, providing a watcher didn't know why the

189

man was there, armed, and why Judith Hudson was also there, a prisoner of Lacey Shafter.

Lou drew his six-gun, looked across, and nodded at Jim. He raised the gun. At that precise moment Judith looked up. She saw the gun and the dingy face and form behind it. She didn't blink or drop a stitch, but gazed out the window for a moment, then, putting aside her knitting, she arose, saying something to the guard about needing a little fresh air, and moved casually over to raise the sash.

Lou eased off, flattening against the wall. All he saw of Judith Hudson, his mother, was a hand upon the bottom of the window sash, lifting it. Then she turned and resumed her seat. When next she spoke, the words came out perfectly to where Lou and Jim were standing.

"Isn't that better?"

The cowboy didn't reply exactly; he grunted, looked around once, then began idly rocking his chair. Lou stepped up, lay his six-gun across the sill, and said: "Mister, you so much as move a finger and you're dead!"

The chair ground abruptly to a halt. The guard's fingers turned white, he gripped his carbine so tightly, but he didn't move, didn't even seem to breathe for a moment. Jim eased the front door open, and stepped inside. Judith Hudson went right on with her knitting, looked up as impassively as before, but with her fingers still moving over and under, the needles making their monotonous little *clicking* sounds.

190

Jim took the cowboy's carbine, then the man's belt gun. "Stand up," he ordered. The cowboy obeyed, stony-faced and bleak. Jim went over him for a hide-out, found nothing, and said: "Come on in, Lou."

Bellanger entered. That was when Judith stopped knitting, carefully put her things aside, and looked at Lou. "You're tired, Son," she said, and slowly got to her feet. "I'll get you something to eat."

"No time," said Lou. "Are you all right?"

She nodded. She was unharmed, she said, but she was anxious about the children and Jamie. Lou holstered his weapon. He told her he thought no one would harm Jamie or the children. Then he asked her why Shafter had brought her out here. Her reply was in line with what Lou and Jim had already figured out for themselves.

"We gave him the deed to the land when he brought the children back, Louis, but he said he'd hold me hostage to be certain Jamie and our friends in town kept quiet. Just before the fight started back a while, he said he was going to send me back to town alone, that he figured none of us would tell how we'd been forced into signing over the land because, if we did, he'd still be able to send gunmen to take care of us."

"You'd never have gotten to town," stated Jim London, holstering his six-gun and stepping over in front of the Mexican Hat cowboy, making a close study of the man's features. "You were one of them that rode into town yesterday with Shafter. I recognize you."

The cowboy was sullen. "All right, London," he growled, laying heavy emphasis on Jim's name to let it be known he knew with whom he was talking. "What'll that prove? Ain't no law says a man can't back up his boss when there's trouble."

"Trouble?" said Jim quietly. "Mister, I don't think you know what trouble is. This here lady you stole from town, now there's *real* trouble. Did you know there's a law against taking folks out of houses at gun point against their will? It's called abduction, and, when it involves females, cowboy, it's just about all the trouble you'll need for maybe ten years . . . in prison."

The cowboy made a tough smile. "You're a hell of a one to talk about prison, London. You've got your picture on half a dozen Wanted posters. Playin' sheriff around here don't change none of that."

Jim didn't argue. All he said was: "Friend, something I learned a long while back. You got to catch a chicken before you can pluck it, and in the meantime a chicken can do a lot of peckin' and scratchin'." Jim turned. "You ready, Lou?"

Bellanger was ready to leave, so was Judith Hudson. Jim reached and gave their captive a light shove toward the door.

Judith was the last one out. She went back to place her knitting carefully in a basket and blow out the lamp. Then she joined the others on the porch and went down to the barn with them.

There were only two saddles, so Lou decided Jim and Judith would ride those, while he rode the Mexican Hat horse, and this left their sullen, embittered captive to ride bareback. In this fashion they left the Hudson place, skirting far northward and heading toward town in a huge half circle that carried them well out of the reach of any stray riders for Lacey Shafter.

Dawn was breaking when they finally sighted the town. For once, the strengthening brightness of new day was their friend; it permitted them to see clearly in all directions. There was no sign of Mexican Hat.

"Found our horses and headed back madder'n hornets," surmised Jim, leading the way straight down into town. At the jailhouse they stopped long enough to throw the prisoner into the cell occupied by that other Mexican Hat rider, then they left Judith in the office while they took the horses down to the livery barn where they wanted to ask some questions.

They almost didn't get a chance to ask them. The minute that troubled night hawk saw them walk in, he dropped his pitchfork and ran forward. "Hey, what in the hell's goin' on around here?" he demanded. "Last night you fellers said you was leavin' the country, an' only about an hour back your saddle animals come chargin' right into the barn with no one on their backs, and twenty minutes after that happened, here come Mister Shafter of Mexican Hat Ranch, and a passel of gun-totin' cowboys kickin' up a hell of a fuss when they seen them horses had no riders on 'em."

Jim held up a hand to silence this torrent of words. "What did Shafter do after he saw our riderless horses?"

"Do?" exclaimed the night hawk, rolling up his eyes. "He liked to had a stroke right here in the center o' the barn, then he commenced cussin' somethin' fierce an' told his men they'd been tricked, to head straight back where they come from on the fly. Them boys went spurrin' away like the end o' the world was comin', leavin' me standin' here with my open mouth hangin' down, holdin' the reins of them horses of yours."

Lou solemnly handed over the reins to the other horses. "Put these up, too," he said. "Let's go, Jim." They got turned around toward the roadway and that was all, before the night hawk jumped at them again.

"Wait a minute, now, consarn it all. Sheriff, them fellers was out to kill someone. I don't want to get mixed up in nothin' like happened out there in the roadway yesterday."

Jim impassively dug out a fat pad of paper money. "How much to feed and stall the horses," he asked, "all of them?"

"Well, I reckon about three dollars, Sheriff. But . . ."

"Here's ten dollars," said Jim, handing the hostler a bill. "Will that take care of the horses, and your loss of sleep an' bein' so upset an' all?"

The hostler's mouth snapped closed while he gazed at the bill. He reached diffidently and took it. For the first time, he lost his worried expression and smiled. "Sheriff," he said stoutly, "that'll take care o' any more lost sleep for a week." He pocketed the bill, broadly smiling. "In fact, Sheriff, that'll keep me from askin' questions, too. I'm mightily obliged to you."

Jim nodded, stepped around the hostler, and went strolling back up the dawn-lighted plank walk with Lou at his side. When they were 100 feet away, Lou said: "We'd better go over an' get Jamie, the kids, and those other folks who were helping the Hudsons, and fetch

194

them all back to the jailhouse, Jim. When Shafter gets to the ranch out there, finds Miz Hudson gone, he's goin' to come back here like a bear with a can tied to his tail."

Neither of them thought at the time that this decision would be a fateful one. The reason they didn't think so was elemental: they'd called all the shots correctly thus far concerning Lacey Shafter. More than ever they had reason to believe Shafter would rush back to the Hudson place to protect his hostage. Even the liveryman had verified that Shafter had told his men to head back, and had even led them westward from the livery barn. The trouble was that Lacey Shafter was also a shrewd man. Part way back it dawned on him that he couldn't possibly reach the Hudson place in time to catch Bellanger and London, so he'd halted his men, considered what Lou and Jim might try after they'd saved Mrs. Hudson, then turned his men around and headed straight back to town. He had one chance left to salvage his scheme, and that was to get the Hudsons' children again, and perhaps Jamie himself, as new hostages.

When Jim and Lou veered off at the intersecting roadway, heading across through the dawn chill, they heard riders, but they seemed to be over east of town, and they were riding slowly, so neither man paid much attention. They went down past the darkened houses toward the small residence where Jamie was, with his children and friends, and were surprised to see Dr. Hart coming out the front door as they approached.

195

Hart seemed just as surprised to see Lou and Jim. He met them at the gate, holding his little black satchel.

With a sinking heart Lou asked if someone was injured. Hart shook his head. "Head cold," he said. "You can't tote children around without wraps on in the night and not expect colds this time of year." Hart squinted. "Did you find Judith? They told me inside what's been happening."

"She's over at the jailhouse," said Jim London. "Tell me something, Doc. How's Jamie?"

Hart's normally unsmiling features loosened. "It's a miracle, that's what it is," he said. "I tell you frankly, Sheriff, I've never privately had much hope for him. But he's been getting to make more and more sense as the hours pass. It's incredible."

Jim nodded soberly. "We're goin' to take him and the kids down to the jailhouse for safe keepin'. We've outfoxed Mexican Hat so far, and, if we can just get everyone Shafter's after down there and securely locked in where no one can get at them, I reckon we can settle the score right soon afterward."

Dr. Hart stood a moment in thought, then shifted his satchel from one hand to the other, and opened the little gate. "I'll help," he said. "You won't need me, I know, but all the same I'll go along."

He led them back to the porch, knocked on the door, and, when the old white-thatched man opened the door with a dragoon-pistol cocked and pointed, Dr. Hart reached over and gingerly pushed that yawning barrel away. "We're all going down to the jailhouse," he announced. "The sheriff and Mister Bellanger have Judith down there."

The old man's screwed up, truculent look vanished. He turned. "Hey, Jamie, come on out here!" He then pushed the big pistol into his waistband and stepped back to permit Hart, Bellanger, and Jim London to step into his darkened, small parlor.

Jamie came ambling in from the back of the house. He saw Jim and Lou at once, smiled, and quickened his step, looking anxiously into the faces of the younger men. "Judith . . . ?" he whispered. "They took Judith away."

Lou said softly: "She's all right. We brought her back. Get the kids, Jamie. We'll take you all down where she is."

Jamie's eyes blazed with sudden light. He turned and ran out of the room followed by the white-haired man. Conrad Hart smiled and sighed, then wagged his head.

CHAPTER
EIGHTEEN

Jim London stepped out on to the front porch, and a man over in shadows at the side of the house jumped out flourishing a gun. "You old goat," he snarled, mistaking Jim for either Jamie or the elderly man who owned the house, "turn right around and go on back inside. Mister Shafter wants to talk to you."

Jim's right hand dipped and rose with the speed of a striking rattler. The astonished man over near the side of the house already had his own gun out, but it wasn't cocked. He may have realized his terrible mistake, and he may not have realized it, but before he could cock his gun, Jim fired. The stranger let out a squawk and went stumbling backward several feet before he dropped his .45 and collapsed.

The others were crowding out when Jim turned, telling them briskly to get back inside. Someone around back cried out. No one ever knew who did that, or why, but it was a safe assumption that one of Shafter's men either in the back alley or in the rear yard saw that man go down, and cried a warning.

Lou whirled, drawing his gun, and ran swiftly into the back of the house, into the sparse little kitchen where it was as dark as the inside of a well. He had no

198

time to speculate on how this had happened; all he had time to understand solidly was that somehow Lacey Shafter, with his hired gunfighters and what remained of his Mexican Hat cowboys, was out back.

A blast of angry gunfire erupted alongside the house. Jim came into the kitchen, gun in hand. "You all set?" he asked, and Lou nodded, twisting to stand beside a window where he could see out. "That's good, because all hell's busted loose over where Shafter's men can see that feller I plugged on the west side of the house."

Lou saw three men stealthily slip into the yard from out back. "Come here," he said, then pointed when Jim stepped across. "I wonder if they know yet someone's filed the firing pins on their guns." He eased up the window, shoved out his .45, and drilled one of those skulking shadows out there plumb center. At once the surviving two men opened up, peppering the back of the house until the sound of tearing wood and breaking glass was an almost constant sound.

When the return fire dwindled, Jim said dryly — "They know." — and eased over to take Lou's place at the window. He drilled two fast shots into some weeds back by the alley fence, jumped back with his pistol raised, and waited. When the angry return fire came that time, Jim stood fast for a moment, then jumped around and shoved his six-gun straight out. Lou was beside him. They sighted both muzzle blasts where their gunfighting enemies were crouching and blazed away. The entire thunderous battle was fought right there for about fifteen long seconds, then it stopped as

199

abruptly as it had begun. Two dead men lay out there under the steely dawn sky, faces down and unmoving.

Jim stepped back to reload. Lou also stepped back and drew fresh cartridges from his shell belt. As they were at it, somewhere in another room that old buffalo carbine cut loose. Every intact window in the little house wildly vibrated, as did the very walls themselves. Carbines opened up in reply, and Lou swung across the room going in search of the old man with his single-shot cannon. He'd be no match for Shafter's men out there with repeating weapons.

The old man was no match, with or without his gun; he'd been creased over the very top of his head. When Lou barged into the room two half-grown children and a small, bird-like elderly woman were struggling to lift him away from the broken, splintered window where he'd fallen across his old gun. Lou stepped across, hoisted the old man, and carried him into a protected corner where a bed stood. He then stepped back beside that same window and waited for the last few bullets to smash on through. Then he dropped down, shoved out his reloaded six-gun, and fired twice at one muzzle blast and fired just once at another muzzle blast. Then he stood up, vaulted through the window, and swung to blaze away at a fleeing figure, but the target dived headfirst through an intervening hedge and was lost to sight.

A cowboy sat on the ground, moaning and holding onto a smashed upper leg. Lou ran past him. Another injured man saw Lou charging and flung away his gun, raising both arms in token of surrender. Lou looked at

200

that one, too, and went past straight for the hedge. Someone behind him sang out, calling his name. He didn't even look back.

There was no more gunfire back at the little house. While the fight had lasted, which couldn't have been more than two or three minutes, several men had fallen and the house itself was badly shot up, but evidently all that was past now because only the sound of Jim London's calling Lou's name came from back there.

Beyond that hedge, through which Lou's adversary had dived, was another small house. This one sat back in the very center of a large lot, surrounded by grass and flowering shrubs. Lou glanced up as he burst through the hedge and saw Elmer Beadle's startled, tousled face peering out at him from a window. He kicked on through and went in a long-legged lope around the back of the house.

His adversary was waiting, and fired. The bullet tore the back out of Lou's shirt. He wrenched half around and fired at the shrubbery up front where the ambusher had been. The man was beating his way frantically through the shrubbery toward the front roadway. Lou wasted one more shot, then hastened forward, taking this fresh course. His adversary got through and over a fence, turned, and threw a wild shot backward, then went sprinting up the roadway keeping close to the fences on the north side.

Lou was slower getting to the roadway, but he made it in time to see his enemy whip around into the main thoroughfare and pass from sight. Lou was built for running on foot, although, like all range men, he had done but very little of this kind of running in his life and had no taste for it even now when it was necessary. But he opened up as soon as he was in the open and reached the far corner. There, he slammed back to a sliding halt. He'd been ambushed before and this was an excellent place for the same thing to happen again.

Across the road, however, old Sam Chavez was standing in the dim dawn light of his doorway, pointing northward. "That way!" he called over, then ducked back inside to get his own gun and join the chase.

Lou didn't wait. He gave a big jump, landed past the cornering buildings, and swung his gun from side to side. The ambusher was not to be seen. Lou stepped forward one step, then sucked back. The gunshot sounded as though it came from halfway up toward Conrad Hart's residence. The bullet tore into wood siding where Lou would have been standing if he hadn't sucked back. For Lou, it had been a ruse, and it had now been a successful one; all he'd intended to do was to bait his adversary into firing. As soon as he knew about where he was, he darted crookedly across the road, was missed by two other fast shots, and threw himself against the front of a store, panting hard.

For a moment there wasn't a sound anywhere. Townsmen in the act of arising were held, still and motionless, wherever they were by this sudden eruption of a savage gunfight outside. Only a complaining milk cow bawled her displeasure somewhere behind the town, and on the east side somewhere a foolish rooster crowed.

"Lou! I'm going around to the north to cut him off. You stay close where you are!"

It was Jim London coming around the same corner where Lou had been earlier. He started to call back, when a flurry of fast shots broke out up the roadway. Both Lou and Jim paused to consider this. As far as they knew, Dr. Hart and Jamie were still back at the little house. Then a tough-sounding harsh voice called out, settling this minor mystery.

"Bellanger! London! He's up here. This is Bob Nichol from Doc's house. Shafter's up here!"

Jim dashed wildly across the road, threw himself up next to Lou, and gasped out his suggestion that they make a charge for Hart's place, keeping under the sidewalk overhangs where darkness hadn't yet been entirely routed by dawn. Lou led off. Jim was short-winded for this kind of work but he gamely hung in there. Another fast exchange of gunshots erupted. Evidently Sheriff Nichol was pinning Lacey Shafter down so that he couldn't flee.

Lou stopped at the edge of a building with a vacant lot on its north side. Jim only hesitated, then sprinted straight on. The second house beyond was Conrad Hart's place. There, when Lou caught up, Bob Nichol, leaning out a window with his smoking six-gun in hand, gestured toward a tall wooden fence at the back of Hart's rear yard. Lou walked up to the very edge of the house, leaned out, and at once a gun flashed viciously from the back. The bullet tore a great chunk out of the siding several inches above Lou's head.

Jim eased up, got down on one knee, poked his six-gun around, then said: "When I cut loose, run!" He fired once, twice, three times, while Lou jumped out into the clear and ran toward the back fence. A gun blazed at him from farther up the fence. Evidently Shafter was seeking to crawl clear by going as far up the yard as he could get. Lou whipped half around and blazed a shot straight at the muzzle blast up there. A man cried out, then subsided with a gasp. The echoes hadn't all died when Lou saw Shafter fold over and fall.

"Got him!" he called back to Jim. "But watch him!"

They both walked forward, guns up, stepping carefully. Elsewhere, men's harsh, aroused voices were being raised indignantly around on the main roadway. Brigham was coming to angry life at last.

Lou halted, reached forward with the toe of his boot, and prodded Lacey Shafter. The cowman moved soddenly and groaned. Lou put up his weapon and knelt. Jim, also, got down to see. Shafter had been hard hit high in the chest. He probably wouldn't make it. Someone padded up behind them. It was Bob Nichol, trailing his six-gun in one hand. "Dead?" he asked dryly.

Lou rocked back and stood up. "No, but hard hit, Sheriff."

"It's Shafter, isn't it?"

"Yes, it's Shafter . . . the damned fool."

"Doc told me he'd imported three gunslingers."

"They're back at the little house where all this started," explained Jim London, arising and dusting off his knees. "Dead."

204

Sam Chavez came around into the yard with his six-gun in its holster. He looked downward and shook his head without making any comment. Lou turned. "Sam, go fetch Doc Hart, will you? Shafter's still breathin'."

Chavez looked at the sprawled body, then up at Lou. "You mean it?" he asked incredulously. "You'd save his life?"

Lou said: "No, Sam, not me. Not Jim. Maybe not you. But the doctor would. His job's different than mine."

Chavez looked at Bob Nichol, raised his shoulders, dropped them, turned, and went shuffling back the way he'd come.

Jim London slowly refilled his six-gun, holstered it, and just as slowly removed the badge from his coat, turned, and pinned it on Bob Nichol's bathrobe. "Never really was mine, anyway," he said, and offered his hand. "It's a good town, Sheriff. I reckon you've made it that way. I've been right proud to pass through it."

Nichol's granite features loosened a little. He shook Two-Gun Jim London's hand and dropped it. "Any time you're up this way, I'd feel right proud if you'd stop by an' have a drink with me, Mister Landon."

A little crowd of curious, puffy-eyed townsmen came edging into the yard. Sheriff Nichol turned and growled. The townsmen vanished back out of the doctor's rear yard. Nichol turned to Lou.

"You, Bellanger . . . ?" he said.

Lou leathered his gun, also, and shoved out his fist. "Me, too, Sheriff."

"Wait a minute," said Jim London, looking troubled. "Lou, you got a reason for stay . . ."

"You got a big mouth," broke in Lou hastily. "I'm ridin' south, Jim. Care to trail along? This is all over but pickin' up the pieces."

London stood frowning at Lou Bellanger for a moment, then he gave his head one hard wag and said: "Sure, this time o' the year they tell me it's right warm and pleasant down around Tombstone. *Adiós*, Sheriff."

"*Adiós*, Mister Landon."

Lou stepped up, hesitated, and said: "Sheriff Nichol, you'll sort of make certain Miz Hudson and Jamie, and their kids are looked out for?"

"You have my word on it," said Bob Nichol. "But wouldn't it be better if you boys . . . ?"

"No," said Lou quickly. "Just tell 'em we had to get on south. Good luck, Sheriff."

"Same to you, son. Same to you."

They shouldered their way through the silent, big-eyed mob of people and ran straight into Sam Chavez returning with Dr. Hart. They moved aside and Dr. Hart nodded and sped on past, but old Sam paused, eyeing them. He didn't say a word though, possibly because of all the people standing close by. Sam just raised a dark hand to his head in a little salute. They smiled and returned that little salute, then walked on.

People were belatedly rushing forward up through town, passing London and Bellanger, scarcely heeding them at all in their haste to get up to where rumor had it someone had been shot down in Conrad Hart's back yard. They got all the way down to the jailhouse, and there Lou's cadenced pacing blurred just for a fraction of a second, then he paced resolutely along beside Two-Gun Jim London.

He didn't look back. It was undoubtedly just as well that he didn't. A wan, gray little woman with large, soft blue eyes was watching from a grilled jailhouse office window. She was holding a pathetically balled-up little cloth handkerchief in one small, work-roughened fist.

Down at the livery barn the night hawk was just turning his duties over to the day man. He turned and smiled when Lou and Jim walked in. "I'll get your horses," he said, and darted away. The day man ignored Jim and Lou to walk out and crane up the roadway toward the yonder excitement.

When their horses came, both men mounted and reined out into the roadway. The night hawk facetiously said — "Well, I reckon you fellers won't be back." — and gave them an exaggerated wink. Lou looked down and said nothing. Jim solemnly returned that wink and said: "Right again. Pardner, you're right again."

They reined southward on to the stage road, booted their animals over into a lope, and rode a full mile, until Brigham was small and blurry in the dawn light, before they slowed and Jim said: "You know, I'd still like to have someone tell me who the hell fired that shot over east of the ranch when we had those two scissor-bills backed up against the Hudsons' corrals."

Lou looked down his nose. "Hell, a kid could figure that out. Remember the feller I knocked silly and we tied up over there? Well, he worked loose, found his gun where you tossed it, and fired to warn Shafter we were around."

Jim began making a cigarette while he considered this. After he'd lit up, he nodded. "All right, I'm not goin' to try to prove you wrong. I never saw a country where so many folks wanted to push lead down my throat before." He whistled a few bars of "Shenandoah", stopped and said: "A pair of aces, that's what we are, Lou. A pair of aces."

Lou smiled. "We were holding the ace card."

The sun jumped up, burnishing the southward world to a rich golden hue. Brigham dropped away behind them, and they rode along whistling, not always in close unison, the song, "Shenandoah".

About the Author

Lauran Paine who, under his own name and various pseudonyms, has written over nine hundred books, was born in Duluth, Minnesota, a descendant of the Revolutionary War patriot and author, Thomas Paine. His family moved to California when he was at a young age and his apprenticeship as a Western writer came about through the years he spent in the livestock trade, rodeos, and even motion pictures where he served as an extra because of his expert horsemanship in several films starring movie cowboy Johnny Mack Brown. In the late 1930s, Paine trapped wild horses in northern Arizona and even, for a time, worked as a professional farrier. Paine came to know the Old West through the eyes of many who had been born in the previous century, and he learned that Western life had been very different from the way it was portrayed on the screen. "I knew men who had killed other men," he later recalled. "But they were the exceptions. Prior to and during the Depression, people were just too busy eking out an existence to indulge in Saturday-night brawls." He served in the U.S. Navy in the Second World War and began writing for Western pulp magazines following his discharge. It is interesting to note that all of his earliest novels (written under his own name and the pseudonym Mark Carrel) were published in the British market and he soon had as strong a following in that country as in the United States. Paine's Western fiction is characterized by strong plots, authenticity, an apparently effortless ability to construct situation and character, and a preference for building his stories upon a solid foundation of historical fact. *Adobe Empire* (1956), one of his best novels, is a fictionalized account of the last twenty years in the life of trader William Bent and, in an off-trail way, has a melancholy, bittersweet texture that is not easily forgotten. In later novels like *The White Bird* (Five Star Westerns, 1997) and *Cache Cañon* (Five Star Westerns, 1998), he has shown that the special magic and power of his stories and characters have only matured along with his basic themes of changing times, changing attitudes, learning from experience, respecting nature, and the yearning for a simpler, more moderate way of life. His next Five Star Western will be *Feud on the Mesa*.